Traitors Among *Dragons*

Maiden to the Dragon, Book 4

Mac Flynn

All names, places, and events depicted in this book are fictional and products of the author's imagination.

No part of this publication may be reproduced, stored in a retrieval system, converted to another format, or transmitted in any form without explicit, written permission from the publisher of this work. For information regarding redistribution or to contact the author, write to the publisher at the following address.

Crescent Moon Studios, Inc.
P.O. Box 117
Riverside, WA 98849

Website: www.macflynn.com
Email: mac@macflynn.com

ISBN / EAN-13: 9781791893040

Copyright © 2018 by Mac Flynn

First Edition

CONTENTS

Chapter 1..1
Chapter 2..10
Chapter 3..16
Chapter 4..24
Chapter 5..30
Chapter 6..40
Chapter 7..48
Chapter 8..55
Chapter 9..62
Chapter 10..70
Chapter 11..76
Chapter 12..82
Chapter 13..89
Chapter 14..95
Chapter 15..102
Chapter 16..109
Chapter 17..117
Chapter 18..124
Chapter 19..131
Chapter 20..139

Continue the adventure..................................146
Other series by Mac Flynn............................153

TRAITORS AMONG DRAGONS

CHAPTER 1

"Pull, My Lady, pull!"
"I'm pulling! I'm pulling!"
"You nearly have it, Miriam!"
"Give me some room!" I snapped.

There I was on the deck of the royal ship in the middle of the lake. It was three weeks after our adventures in the labyrinth, and I was taking some time to learn the intricacies of the cuisine. Behind me were Magnus and Darda, and in front of me was the wide expanse of waters. I held a fishing pole in my hands and determination on my face.

Magnus and Darda stepped back. I yanked back the fishing pole and spun another few feet of horse-hair line around the hook at the base of the wooden stick. The stick bent over the railing and brushed the waves that rocked the ship. A silver fish broke the surface and sailed over the waves before it splashed back into the water. I gritted my teeth and gave a hard pull of the rod with both hands.

The fish flew out of the water and landed with a hard slap onto the deck of the ship. It flopped about before Magnus threw a net over the flopping behemoth. Its large silver belly shimmered in the warm afternoon sun.

Magnus stepped up and grinned over my prey. "A nice one, My Lady. A good two pygme, if Ah'm not a daktylos off. The god of the lake smiles on you."

I blinked at him before I looked to Darda. "Is that good?"

She smiled and nodded. "The measurement is nearly equal to thirty inches."

I straightened and grinned. "That's good enough for me."

Magnus nodded. "Aye, tis a good fish. My Lord and ya will eat well tonight."

I turned away at the glistening castle set against the hillside. It was a glistening crown to the large white city at my back. The spires cast their long shadows over the rippling waters of the large lake that separated the capital from the residence of its lord, Xander, and its beautiful, majestic lady, namely me.

A soft smile slipped onto my lips. "Let's see that dragon eat *this* all by himself."

The old captain chuckled. "Ah won't be counting my cargo the ship's come to port, My Lady." He looked over his shoulder at the helm. Nimeni, his pale first mate, stood behind the wheel. "Back to the castle!"

Nimeni nodded and aimed the bow to the castle. We sailed over the deep blue waters of Lake Beriadan and toward the long dock of the castle. I set my hands on the railing and looked into the water. My distorted reflection stared back at me, but far below that was a band of blue light that flitted alongside the boat. I grinned and waved. It flicked its tail before it dove into the black depths of the deep lake.

We arrived at the dock, and my catch and I were escorted into the castle. My dragon lord, the annoyingly handsome Xander, met us in the courtyard. His eyes immediately fell on the fish in the arms of the castle guard. "The gods were kind to you this day."

"I only needed one, and a little skill," I told him.

He smiled. "An unfortunate combination for the fish. Shall we consume it tonight?"

I grinned. "I was thinking about parading it around a little longer, but-" I pinched my nose shut, "-I think it's already starting to smell."

Xander chuckled as he nodded at the guard who left us. "Then we will feast tonight, and enjoy one another's company later in the evening."

I sidled up to him and leaned against him. "Are you sure you can make time in your busy kingdom-running schedule for me?" His face fell. I winced. "Bad news?"

He wrapped his arm around my waist and shook his head. "No, something far worse."

My heart dropped into my stomach as I looked into his crestfallen face. "You're going away again?"

Xander turned to me and clasped my hands. A smile teased the corners of his lips. "No, my Miriam. Bucephalus and I will not leave your side for a long while yet. What concerns me is the Bestia that attacked you, and the raid on the south."

I arched an eyebrow. "You think they're connected?"

He nodded. "I do. The raid led me away from my city when it most needed me, and the Bestia who attacked the south took nothing of value from the poor villages. Thus we may assume they meant for me not to be present during their search for Bucephalus."

I grinned. "But I was."

Xander leaned forward and pecked a teasing kiss on my lips. He leaned back and studied my eyes with a true smile. "Yes, and I owe you my city for it."

"How about just saving me a piece of that fish?" I teased.

Xander straightened and bowed his head. "I will do as you command, and more."

As it turned out he couldn't keep his promise, but that wasn't his fault. The supper hour came, a late one at seven o'clock. Xander and I sat at the long table in the large dining hall with a row of servants standing at the ready should we need another fork or a bib. I was seated on his left and in front of us was a fortune's worth of silverware. The silver fish was presented to us on a silver platter.

Xander picked up his fork and knife, and smiled at me. "May I offer you a fin, or perhaps the tail?"

I snorted. "You really like to eat like a king here, don't you?"

He chuckled as he carved a hearty portion from the fish and slid it onto my plate. "It is the company that gives me such an appetite, and the nightly exercise."

I picked up my own utensils and sliced into the fish. I held up the slice and grinned at him over the piece. "You could say you caught yourself a perfect Maiden."

Xander placed a large slice on his plate and grinned. "And I have you as proof my victory was not a fish story."

TRAITORS AMONG DRAGONS

Our tug-of-war with puns ended with the entrance of Tillit. The sus sauntered into the room and took for himself the chair opposite me. "Good evening, my favorite dragon lord and Maiden."

Xander arched an eyebrow as he studied our unexpected guest. "You did not bribe the guards to allow you entrance again, did you?"

Tillit grinned as he shook his head. "Nope. I'm actually here on official business." He reached into his coat and drew out an envelope which he held out to Xander. "I was with Kinos when this came up to the front gate. They were swamped out there-you really need to add another gate-so he asked me to give it to you."

Xander took the envelope and opened it while Tillit looked at the fish on my plate. "It looks like Beriadan's still rewarding you for saving his city."

I frowned and wagged my knife at him. "There was some skill involved, too."

He chuckled, but the mirth died on his lips when he glanced at Xander's strained face. "No good news from the Heavy Mountains?"

Xander shook his head as he broached the contents of the letter again. "No. On the contrary, Herod wishes for my assistance, and that I travel to his realm immediately."

Tillit gave off a piggish snort. "If that's true it'll be the first time that prince of darkness asks anyone for help. What's he want help with, anyway?"

"He does not say."

The sus wrinkled his flat nose. "Typical. That guy's more paranoid than any sus I've met, and that's saying something."

Xander folded the note and slipped it back into the envelope before he looked to me. "I fear this will call me away again."

My eyebrows crashed down. "Just you?"

"I did promise you rest for at least a month," he reminded me.

I set my elbow on the table and leaned toward him to look him square in the eyes. "Let's just get this straight: from now on where you go, I go. If there's going to be trouble, I can at least scream so you can fly down and rescue your damsel."

"Can you not whistle?" he wondered.

I snorted. "I can't even breathe through my nose."

He pressed his lips together and gave off a melodious sound. "It is easy."

I leaned back in my chair and folded my arms over my chest. "Not easy enough for me to do it, and I'm kind of hoping I'm not even going to need to scream on this little adventure of ours."

"I will have to teach you some time," he replied as he turned to Tillit. "Can we expect the pleasure of your company on this adventure?"

Tillit stood and shook his head. "This is one adventure I'm staying out of. There's only room enough on that mountain for one sus, and that position's filled. Besides, I've got some business at Bear Bay that might prove lucrative." He turned away, but paused and looked over his shoulder at us. His expression was tense. "Whatever you do up there on that god-forsaken place, just don't get lost. I wouldn't want my best customers bleaching their bones among those stupid rocks."

Xander smiled and bowed his head. "I swear nothing of the sort will happen."

Tillit grinned. "Well, that's better than nothing. Good luck on your trip up that lonely mountain." He strolled from the room, but a wisp of his voice floated behind him. "You're gonna need it. . ."

My eyes flickered to Xander and I jerked my head in the direction Tillit had gone. "*Are* we going to need it?"

Xander took up his knife and fork and sliced into his fish. "Perhaps," he replied as he took a bite.

My face fell. "That doesn't exactly give me comfort."

His eyes looked up from his plate. "Would you rather remain behind?"

I frowned and slumped in my chair. "No, but still-" I couldn't organize my worried thoughts.

Xander set down his utensils and took one of my hands in his. He gave it a gentle squeeze as he smiled at me. "Have I allowed any harm to come to you?"

I furrowed my brow. "Well, now that you mention it there was that one time at the Portal-"

"You returned to me unscathed."

"-and the near-death experience at the ruins in the forest-"

"Death did not even part us."

"-and then you left me to protect the city all by myself-"

Xander leaned forward and pressed a passionate kiss on my lips that heated my body. I groaned into the union and whimpered when he pulled us apart. A mischievous smile slipped onto his lips. "You were saying?"

I glared at him. "I was saying that you play dirty in arguments."

He leaned back in his chair and smiled gently at me. "However devious my actions, know that my intentions toward you will forever me pure."

My shoulders slumped and I sighed. "All right, I'll rehire you as my bodyguard, but don't expect any bonuses while we're there." I furrowed my brow. "And where exactly is 'there,' anyway? And who are we helping exactly?"

"Herod is the dragon lord of the Heavy Mountains, a realm located in the northeastern part of the continent." He looked down at the envelope that lay beside his plate. "It would be a rather long journey on horse, but the urgency of his letter implies we should fly."

I raised an eyebrow. "Like full-dragon fly?"

He shook his head. "No. Though that form is faster in flight, the distance is fully two days away by air. Any in our entourage who is not a lord would perish from the strain on their bodies."

I winced. "Only a day? How long would it take you to-well, you know-"

"Two days before my body, too, would give out," he told me.

"But weren't you guys dragons before? I mean, you haven't always been human looking, have you?" I asked him.

He shook his head. "No, but the days of flight in our dragon bodies are long past. Those with the greatest strength of dragon form perished long ago in wars against the humans and each other. The lines that remain are too weak to retain the form without certain death."

My face fell. "Bummer."

TRAITORS AMONG DRAGONS

Xander smiled at me. "Do not pity us. We still have our wings, and they grant us enough freedom to travel over the continent without too much difficulty. We should arrive at the border of Herod's realm within three days."

"Sounds like the usual terrifying fun. When do we leave?"

"At first light."

CHAPTER 2

"Not so fast!"

The screeching, terrified creature was me. Xander held me in his arms against his chest. My arms were wrapped tightly around his neck. There were a lot of reasons for this, about five hundred, to be exact. Those five hundred reasons were the five hundred feet between us and the ground that we flew over.

"If we go slower we will not reach the base of the Heavy Mountains before nightfall," he told me.

What I hated more than seeing the ground so far down there was *not* seeing the ground because of night. Instead I looked behind us. We were flanked by Spiros on one side and Darda on the other. They carried the bags with our limited supplies on their backs. Beyond them stretched the vast lands that separated us from the distant, long-out-of-sight castle of Alexandria. There was only the four of us way up there.

"Tell me again why we couldn't bring *all* the palace guards," I pleaded.

"Herod requested I bring as few companions as possible," he reminded me.

I raised an eyebrow. "How paranoid is this guy?"

Xander pursed his lips. "He is a very cautious lord. It would do well for you to speak as little as possible so as not to arouse his ire and suspicion."

I leaned away from him and frowned. "What would he think I'm hiding? A plot to overthrow his realm?"

"Such a thought may enter his mind," he warned me.

I looked down at myself and frowned. A thick cloak covered my body, and beneath that was one of the fancy dresses made by the castle seamstress. "And that's why I'm having to wear these stupid dresses?"

"Unfortunately, yes. He is rather old-fashioned, having come from an older generation of dragons."

I snuggled against his warm chest and sighed. "The things I do for adventure in this place. So what do these mountains of his look like, anyway?"

Xander's head perked up and he nodded in the direction ahead of us. "Those are the Heavy Mountains."

I followed his gaze and beheld a range of jagged, snow-capped mountains. They rose up from the forest floor like scabs and pierced the black-clouded sky with their gray, gnarly shapes. Sparse trees covered their steep hillsides, but the slopes were pocketed with boulders and scarred with black patches of roasted rocks.

Among the peaks were tiny valleys of short, stubby trees that crowded around cold creeks. Nestled in one of those valleys, one devoid of trees, was an imposing stone castle. The blackened stone reflected the darkening sky and left me with a chill.

I shivered at the sight and squirmed closer to Xander's body heat. "Cozy looking place, isn't it?"

"They are rather bleak," he admitted.

"Is there a reason they're called the Heavy Mountains? Do they make people feel heavy, or are they trying to tip over the continent?"

He shook his head. "Nothing like that. The name derives from the fact that no dragon may fly over the upper half of the elevation."

I raised an eyebrow. "Why not?"

"It is rather a long story."

I glanced at the many miles between us and the base of the mountains. "I think we've got time."

He took a deep breath. "Four thousand years ago the forests were the realm of the dragons, but the peaks were ruled by humans. Herod's ancestor gathered his forces and marched on the mountains to take the resources. At first they attacked the mountains in their dragon forms, but the humans possessed a great sorcerer. That sorcerer climbed the highest peak and cursed the entire range so that no dragon could fly over the upper half of the elevation."

"What would happen to them?" I asked him.

"Their wings will cease to flap and they would plummet to the earth."

I cringed. "Ouch."

He nodded. "Yes. Herod's ancestor and his army felt a great deal of pain that day. The sorcerer cast the spell at the point when many of the dragons in their full forms flew over the peaks. They fell to their deaths on the rocks below. At the end of the battle the day belonged to Herod's ancestor, but with such loss of life the victory was a hollow one."

"So that was one of the wars that killed off the dragons who could fly in the dragon form?" I guessed.

Xander pursed his lips as he looked out over the cold, gray mountains. "One of many. Far too many."

I cleared my throat. "So where's Herod's place?"

He nodded at the tallest peak. A jagged bunch of smaller peaks made a mess of spiked rocks. "His castle is situated among the stones there."

I furrowed my brow. "But isn't that over halfway up the mountain?"

"Yes, but we will not be flying to the castle. There is a path at the base that grants entrance to those invited by the lord," he told me.

"This guy really is paranoid, isn't he?"

Xander shook his head. "He is merely cautious. The mountains were the last human stronghold to be taken by the dragon lords, and the conquest was not finished for another five hundred years after the castle was taken. During that time, the humans waged an unorthodox war against the dragons wherein they used surprise to attack and any counterattack was met with a retreat into the Coven Caves. A great many humans managed to secretly enter their former castle and murder several prominent dragon warriors, including the lord who had taken their land."

My eyes widened. "Wow. And they kept that up for five hundred years?"

He nodded. "Yes, until the grandson of the murdered lord set fire to the caves and destroyed the remnants of the humans."

I frowned and straightened. "They didn't murder him. They were just trying to get back their castle from the dragon that stole it from them."

Xander smiled. "I recall that my mother said much the same when she first heard the tale. My father and mother had quite an argument, and they did not speak to one another for quite some days."

"So should we carry on tradition or are you going to agree with me?" I wondered.

He chuckled. "We will ignore tradition and end this discussion in an amicable draw."

I grinned. "I accept your surrender."

Xander closed his wings close to his body. We fell into a steep dive toward the forested ground. The wind pulled my hair behind me and whipped at my face with its cold, dry tongue.

I clung to my dragon lord and glared at him. "What the hell are you doing?"

He smiled at me as he opened his wings. The wind caught us and we glided over the tips of the trees. "A dragon lord without honor is nothing. Death would be a better fate."

I rolled my eyes. "Well, if you're going to do that then let me down." His wings tensed. I stuck my face in his and glared at him. "Not that way!"

Xander pecked a teasing kiss on my lips and stretched his wings. "I accept your surrender."

I folded my arms over my chest and slouched in his arms. Spiros flew close to us. "Is all well, My Lord?"

"Merely a tradition," Xander replied.

Spiros looked to me with a mischievous glint in his eyes. "Methinks the lady dislikes this tradition."

TRAITORS AMONG DRAGONS

My narrowed eyes flickered to Xander. "Very much." A sly smile slid onto my lips. "Maybe I should ride with Spiros for a while. You know, for the change of scenery."

Xander's eyebrows crashed down and he clutched me tighter to his chest. "Tradition demands you remain with me, and we are almost at our destination."

We flew over the dark forests with our two companions at our rear. The trees eroded away before the rocky soil of the mountains and all but disappeared a hundred yards from the foot.

The black, rocky slope was scarred by a winding path that disappeared into a patchy fog. The white fog wafted over the large boulders like a snake. At the base of the path was a large archway hewn from a single stone. The arch stretched twenty feet over the mouth of the route. Its face was blackened by fire, but on the surface was carved straight lines and round circles with a few squiggly ones thrown into the mix. Their gray color stood out against the black, even in the dimming light of the day.

It was an entrance Dracula would have been proud to call his own.

CHAPTER 3

Xander landed us twenty feet from the arch. A small stone house stood nearby, and from the building emerged a sus. The man was rough with bristles along his chin and a poorly-cut fur coat over his pudgy body. His tiny eyes flickered from one of us to the other until he settled on Xander.

"What's wanted?" he snarled.

Xander set me down and drew out the letter from Herod which he passed to the sus. "We have an invitation from Lord Herod."

The sus looked over the contents, stretched his snarl, and handed the letter back. "Fine, but you'd better hurry it up the mountain. The weather's going to get bad soon."

TRAITORS AMONG DRAGONS

I looked up at the sky. Black clouds peeked over the tips of the peaks. A chill wind blew down the mountain path and swept past us as though escaping rocks for the forest.

The sus turned away from us and put his fat fingers in his mouth. He blew a whistle that rang off the gray stones. A noise came from behind those same stones. It was the sound of shuffling feet. From behind a few boulders emerged three short, hairy men. They were about four feet tall with long, scruffy brown beards and hair down to their waists. They wore dull brown leather shirts and pants, but their feet were bare and showed off thick, hairy feet. At their waists were leather belts, though the leader of the three had sparkling stones on his wear. Tools were tucked into straps set at intervals in the belts.

The three walked under the arch and over to where we stood. The sus gestured to them. "These dwarves will be your guides. Do exactly as they tell you when they tell you-"

"-otherwise you'll be dead," the scruffiest of the dwarves spoke up.

I winced and let my eyes travel up the steep path. "Isn't there any other way up to the castle?"

The sus shook his head. "No."

Xander grasped my hand and smiled at me. "You forget that I am by your side, and have sworn to protect you."

I returned his smile with one of my own. "And I'm keeping you to that promise."

The lead dwarf sneered and half-turned away from us. He jerked his head toward the path. "Hurry it up. We don't have all day."

The short men guided us to the archway. They passed under without a pause. Xander was halfway through with me a half step behind when my hand in his grasp reached the center of the arch.

I felt like I was struck by lightning. A bolt of energy shot from the walls of the arch and hit my hand. I was thrown back into the arms of Spiros. Xander spun around and hurried over to me.

He grasped my arms as Spiros righted me onto my shaky legs. I grinned up at him. "This Herod guy sure knows how to say hello, doesn't he?"

The sus jogged up to us with his potbelly bouncing up and down. His beady eyes glared at Xander. "What are you trying to pull bringing magic up there?"

Xander's narrowed eyes flickered up to the pig-man. "She is my Maiden."

The sus nodded at me. "I don't care who she is, but whatever she's hiding I need to see it."

I shoved my hand into his face and let the small plume of smoke from the point of impact waft into his nostrils. "There's your magic stuff!"

He stumbled back and wrinkled his hog nose. "What'd she do? Drink it?"

"My Maiden has fae blood within her," Xander informed him as the dwarves joined our little group.

The leader studied me with bushy curiosity. "What kind of fae?"

I cradled my injured hand against my chest. "The bad kind to get through that arch."

The dwarf straightened to his full short height and puffed out his chest. "Nothing magical can get through that archway. It's made with the finest dwarf detection and magic expulsion system. A thimble of magic wouldn't be let through."

TRAITORS AMONG DRAGONS

I studied the arch and the boulders on either side of the columns. "Can't somebody just walk around it?"

He grinned and shook his head. "That won't work. The system goes around the whole of the mountains."

Xander looked to the sus. "Will my Maiden be allowed to pass, or must my party return to Alexandria?"

The sus pursed his lips. "You can pass, but I'm going to have to report this to Herod. I don't need to tell you that he won't be happy about it."

"If he wishes for our assistance he will overlook this minor bending of the rules," Xander replied.

The sus pursed his lips, but turned to the dwarves. "Unlock the arch."

The dwarf scowled in return, but spun around and stalked over to the arch with his two companions. One each took the sides, and the leader took the middle. The two grunts each pulled a chisel and hammer from their belts and set the chisel in one of the grooves. They positioned their hammers over the heads of the chisels and waited.

"Now!" the leader called out.

They struck the chisels at the same time. Two clanging sounds reverberated up the arch and to the top where they met. The noises canceled out one another. The lead dwarf nodded his head and turned to us. "That should do it. Now let's get going."

Xander grasped my hands and led me forward. I felt like a thief trying to walk between a store security checkpoint. The buzzer didn't go off this time and I sailed through with the others. The dwarves repeated their strange ritual and reactivated the invisible barrier. They tucked their tools in their belts and strode past us up the steep slope.

We followed after them which wasn't an easy feat. The dwarves were as nimble as mountain goats. Their bare feet seemed to catch every loose stone and propel them forward. I soon found myself breathing hard against the rough path and the quick pace.

The weather didn't help. Those black clouds blocked out the sun and left us in a dark shadow of cold. The wind didn't let up, but grew colder as it whipped my cloak around me. We were only halfway up the mountain when I felt like a popsicle.

I stuck my cold hands in my pockets. My fingers hit the familiar round object of King Thorontur's soul stone. I winced. Xander's eyes flickered down to me.

He leaned close to me. "What is the matter?"

I bit my lip. "I-um, I was just remembering that present the green guy in the forest gave me. You know, that round one." I nodded at the dwarves ahead of us. "I don't know if they'd like it or not."

His eyes widened for the briefest of moments before he straightened. "I'm sure a skipping stone, even one as impressive as that, won't be of interest to Herod or anyone else."

I nodded and tucked the stone deep into my pocket. That was one magic ace up my sleeve. That is, if I could just figure out how to use it.

I glanced at the rocks on either side of us. Some held deep chips on their surfaces, and four inches beneath the blackness was gray rock. I tugged on Xander's sleeve and nodded at one of the deep breaks. "What's with the different colors?"

"The black's the mark of the dragon," the lead dwarf called back.

TRAITORS AMONG DRAGONS

I raised an eyebrow. "Wouldn't a claw be a better mark?"

The dwarf shook his head without turning around. "Nope. That there is the fire from the dragons that burned this place so they could take what was left of it."

Xander looked at the belt that was looped around the middle of the dwarf leader. "You hold a fine hammer, dwarf."

The leader turned his head to one side and frowned at Xander without missing a step. "I should. It's been in my family for ten generations."

"Then you are of the house of Amram?" Xander asked him.

The dwarf narrowed his eyes. "How did you know that?"

Xander smiled. "As a young dragon I visited the Heavy Mountains and made the acquaintance of Amram. He saved me from a stampede of wild goats, and my father rewarded him with diamonds for his belt."

A ghost of a smile slipped onto the lips of the stern dwarf. "Aye, Ah know of you. My grandpap spoke of a foolish young dragon lord who went into the forbidden valley to hunt goats, and found more than he could handle."

Xander bowed his head. "You have met him."

The dwarf leader fell back to us and held out his hand to Xander. "It's an honor to meet you. My name is Amown, son of Bram."

Xander took the hand and gave it a good shake. "I am Xander, son of Alexander the Tenth."

"What brings you here to this black mountain, son of Alexander?" Amown asked him.

My dragon lord nodded at the path ahead of us. "Herod has requested our help. You wouldn't happen to know with what, would you?"

Amown snorted. "That dragon wouldn't trust his shadow to tell him the time of day."

"But he trusts you with the arch," I pointed out.

"Because he can't do it himself, and won't give all his safety to his sorcerer," Amown told me.

"What sorcerer does he keep now?" Xander asked him.

Amown's bushy eyebrows shot down. "A bad one. He calls himself Mordecai, but Ah reckon that isn't his real name. "

"How many sorcerers has he had?" I spoke up.

"Many, but never more than one at a time," Xander replied.

Amown nodded. "Aye. He grabbed this one ten years ago when his other one died."

"Why would anyone want to work for Herod?" I asked them.

The dwarf frowned. "Herod has his ways of convincing them to work for him. Take us-" he nodded to his fellow dwarves. "Here we are taking care of this trail and the arch, and barely paid a pittance in coins and the mineral rights."

"How are the mines?" Xander wondered.

He pursed his lips and shook his head. "None too good. The silver is running out, and the jewels aren't what they used to be. Ya couldn't find these-" he tapped the jewels on his belt, "-much these days, not even if one's life depended on it."

Xander arched an eyebrow. "Have your people opened new mines?"

TRAITORS AMONG DRAGONS

Amown frowned. "No. Herod won't allow-" The dwarves froze so quickly Xander and I nearly stumbled into the ones in front of us.

Amown's eyes widened and he threw himself onto the ground. The dwarf shoved his ear against the dirt, shut his eyes and held very still.

Xander knelt beside him and spoke in a whisper. "What's the-" The dwarf's eyes flew open and he jumped to his feet so quickly the top of his head nearly collided with Xander's chin. He spun around to face our group.

"Avalanche!"

CHAPTER 4

I heard the rumble a second after Amown's announcement. An earthquake made the pebbles at our feet bounce across the hard-packed dirt.

Amown grabbed Xander and my arms, and pulled us toward the rock wall that lined the path. Spiros and Darda were snatched by the other dwarves and dragged after us.

"Get inside!" Amown ordered us.

I shook my head. "I don't see-" Amown slammed the back of his fist against a sunken rock. The door in the wall sank into the mountain and created a nook. "Oh. That."

"In ya go!" Amown shouted as he pushed us into the nook.

The other two dwarves shoved our companions into another hidden nook that was opposite ours. Our guides pressed our backs against the rear walls as the earthquake and roar grew louder. Xander wrapped his arm around my waist and pressed me close to him. My teeth rattled as small rocks rolled down the path past us. Those small rocks turned to massive boulders that tumbled to the base of the mountain. Dirt and broken bits of stone mixed with the rocks and clouded the air with their powder.

I shut my eyes and choked on the dust as flakes of stone pattered my body. "Hold on! It's almost through!" Amown shouted.

The dwarf's words turned out to be true again as the boulders stopped their tumbling and the earth its shaking. The terrible roar of the avalanche subsided, as did the swirling dust. I opened my eyes and beheld a five-foot wall of stone in front of us. If I stood on my tiptoes I could see over the top. Spiros and Darda, with their dwarven friends, were in the same situation.

"Xander!" Spiros called.

"Still among the living," Xander replied.

"Miriam?" Darda shouted.

"Present, but pale," I answered.

Amown pressed his palms against the rocks just above his head and looked to Xander. His beard was covered in gray dust and his bright eyes stood out from his pale face. "Get on the ground."

Xander blinked at him. "I do not-"

"Just get on your hands on knees," Amown ordered him.

Xander complied with the request and Amown climbed on top of his back. The dwarf pulled out his chisel and hammer, and swept his palm over the rocks on the top of the pile. His eyes lit up on one particular spot, and he set the tip of his chisel on the smooth part of one high boulder. A simple clink against the chisel and the whole of the pile vibrated. The top half of the wall crumbled under the tune of his tools and fell into dust atop the remaining rocks.

I looked to Amown and pointed at the ruin of rock. "How did you do that?"

The spry dwarf stepped off Xander and onto the top of the short pile. He stopped just beyond the wall and turned to us with a crooked grin. "We dwarves know the stones as well as we know our own hands, miss. A sledgehammer in the hands of a dragon cannot move them as much as a tiny nick from a dwarf child."

Xander climbed to his feet and admired the work. "Very well done, son of Bram."

Amown puffed up, but cleared his throat. "Of course it is, but quit your yapping and get over here."

Xander climbed over and turned around where he grabbed my hand and pulled me a pull over the top. The other dwarves performed the same work, and they and our companions clamored over their ruined rock wall. We rejoined in the middle of the ruined path.

I looked up and down the trail. Boulders and rocks littered our way. The archway was buried beneath a small mountain of debris. The sus's cottage was destroyed, but we could see the sus himself at the edge of the tree line and coming in our direction.

I turned to Xander. "Now what?"

"We may be able to glide down the trail," he suggested.

Amown stepped between us and glared at Xander. "Ah'm supposed to get you up the mountain, and Ah mean to do it. The trail is a bit of a wreck, Ah'll admit, but we'll get up it." He looked Xander in the eyes. "Besides, yer expected by Herod, and he's not one to bring someone all this way for nothing."

Xander pursed his lips and looked up the trail. "I must agree, but I worry about my Maiden."

I crossed my arms and frowned at him. "I'm a big girl. I can take care of myself." I glanced at the nook with its wall of stone. "Well, mostly."

Amown crawled over some of the boulders above us and set his chisel to a particularly large one. A single tap turned not only that rock to dust, but all the others within three feet of it so the ground could be seen. The dwarf paused and looked over his shoulder at us. "Well? Are ya coming or not?"

"Coming," Xander replied.

The last half of the journey was a nightmare of boulder climbing and dust choking. The last rays of the setting sun disappeared over the horizon and draped us in night's twinkling stars and blackness. The dwarves were as spry as ever in the darkness, but I slipped and slid over one rough rock after another. One particular fall wedged my leg between two heavy stones.

I twisted around to look to Xander as he came up behind me. "I'm stuck!"

"Remain calm," he soothed as he stooped down near my leg.

Xander pressed his palms against either side of my leg and gritted his teeth as he pushed them apart. My leg loosened enough so I could pull my leg free. I tumbled backward onto my rear and breathed a sighed of relief.

"Please tell me we're almost there," I asked my dragon lord.

Amown, who were a full ten yards ahead of us with his companions, paused and looked to us. "Almost, but you can use this the rest of the way." He pulled out a thick, short stick from his belt. One end was blackened. He struck that end against a nearby stone. The stick lit up like a match and illuminated the area like a lamp.

Xander escorted me over to them and accepted the much-needed gift. I looked from the torch to the dwarf. "Why don't you guys need it?"

Amown grinned and tapped his temple. "We're dwarves, miss. We were born in the darkest caves, and we'll die in them."

"Oh. Right."

Spiros and Darda received torches of their own, and our small fire line followed the sturdy dwarves as they chiseled their way up the path. Xander lifted his torch and studied the untouched rocks on either side of us. "What do you think could have caused the avalanche? A weakness in the trail wall?"

Amown slammed his hammer down hard on his chisel. The reverberations rattled the ground and caused rocks to dust-ify ten feet up the path. He spun around and wagged his chisel at Xander. "Ah won't hear of any of that talk, dragon. The stones on these paths are as reliable as the sun."

"Even the sun is hidden by clouds," Xander returned.

Amown swung his chisel and pointed at some of the stones. His eyes were a smoldering fury. "No sun nor failed wall did this."

"Then what did?" Spiros spoke up.

Amown turned his back on us and set his chisel against a boulder. His eyebrows were so low they nearly covered his eyes. "Ah don't know, but Ah'll find out."

TRAITORS AMONG DRAGONS

We carried onward through the night. A thick fog slithered over us and dampened our dusty bodies. The steep path leveled out near the high peaks and the width of the path widened. We reached the final fifty yards of the path before it reached one of the small valleys nestled in the peaks, and found our way already cleared. The cleaning was thanks to a crew of soldiers clad in black armor. They heaved and tossed the huge stones from the trail, but stepped back when we neared them.

Amown dusted the final boulders in our path and Xander took the lead. He presented himself to a soldier who walked down the path and stopped in front of us. "I am-"

"We were informed of your coming, Lord Xander," the soldier replied. He stepped aside and gestured to the crest of the trail. "If you would follow me." He glanced at the dwarves and pursed his lips. "You are also to come along."

Amown frowned, but pocketed his tools and nodded. Our group followed the soldier up the path to the head of the trail. The peaks and fog parted and opened to reveal a small, bowl-shaped valley in the middle of the craggy stones. Short, stubby pine trees grew in the shallow soil and lined the gravel path that led from where we stood to the single gateway of a large stone castle. Its jagged towers resembled the peaks that surrounded it, and thick walls were guarded by soldiers that marched atop their battlements. The huge gates were hewn from two large trees, and were tightly shut to us.

Several other gaps in the peaks on either sides of the valley indicated other trails, but the soldier gestured to the castle below us.

"This way. My lord awaits us."

CHAPTER 5

The soldier led us down the gravel path to the high gates of the castle. A rumbling from the clouds warned us the darkness wasn't all for show. A few random raindrops hit my head, and the scent of water filled the air.

As we approached the castle I noticed the foundation ruins of several smaller buildings. I tugged on Xander's arm and nodded at the rocks. "What were those?"

"A village once stood near the castle, but Lord Herod's ancestors grew wary of the inhabitants and ordered them away," he told me.

"Nice fellows. . ." I murmured as we reached the gates.

The rough gray stone of the walls mirrored the hard looks given to us by the guards that stood watch on the battlements. The soldier raised his hand and a heavy clanking noise resounded from the other side.

TRAITORS AMONG DRAGONS

The gates creaked open and revealed a large courtyard with a stone ground. The three other sides of the courtyard were surrounded by tall walls with narrow slits for windows. Only a single pair of doors that stood opposite the gate led into the castle.

I leaned toward Xander. "These dragon guys are really serious about their security, aren't they?"

His eyes flickered to the guards positioned at intervals on the walls. They stared back with equal intensity. "Yes, but I feel something is amiss-"

"Miriam!" a voice yelled. Movement in one of the second floor windows caught my eye. A hand waved at me before it retracted and was replaced by the familiar face of Olivia, my 'friend' from the Maiden ritual. "Up here!" I gave a weak smile and a wave.

The doors of the castle swung open and out marched a contingent of guards. At the head of the group was the dark lord himself, Herod. He wore a suit of polished black armor that glistened in the starlight. His heavy boots clapped against the stones in time with the guards behind him. Draped over his shoulders and flowing behind him was a long cape that, when he stopped in front of us, settled against his back down to his ankles. He walked with a slight limp.

At his side was a white-bearded man of fifty. The fellow wore a black robe over a black shirt and pants. The pants were tucked into black boots. The only deviation from the monochrome scheme was a red band wrapped around the lower part of his neck.

Herod's dark eyes looked over our faces until they stopped on Xander. "I instructed that only you should come. Who are these others?"

"Nice welcome. . ." I muttered.

Xander shot me a warning glance before he nodded at Spiros. "This man is my captain. You would not have me do without my own protection, would you, Lord Herod?"

Herod's frown deepened as his eyes flickered to Darda and me. "Are these women also for your protection?"

Darda stepped forward and bowed low to the lord. "We are, Your Lordship." I looked at her like she was nuts.

Herod arched an eyebrow and lifted his peaked nose. "Is the city of Alexandria so lacking in men that they resort to-" Darda slipped forward and whipped out a knife from her robes. The end of the blade swept close to Herod's neck and might have nicked him if he hadn't leaned back.

His guards leapt forward and drew their claws from their human hands. A dozen talons pressed against various points of Darda's own throat. Spiros grasped the hilt of his sword, but Xander set his hand atop that of his friend. The robed man's eyes flickered over our faces, but otherwise he didn't move an inch.

A mirthless chuckle interrupted the tense scene. Herod raised his hand. The guards drew back and their talons changed back to fingers. He looked to Xander. "You have an impressive servant, Lord Xander."

A crooked smile slipped onto Xander's lips. "More than you know."

"More than I knew. . ." I muttered as Darda slipped behind me. I glanced over my shoulder at her, but her head was bowed and her eyes were riveted to the ground.

"You must be fatigued from your journey," Herod added. He stepped aside and the guards behind him parted into two rows with a path between them. Our host swept his arm toward the doors. "You will be shown to your rooms.

TRAITORS AMONG DRAGONS

Dinner will be served in a half hour, and at that time I will inform you of why I requested your presence."

Xander nodded at his leg. "Your leg appears to trouble you, Lord Herod. What is the matter?"

Herod's face darkened. "It was a riding accident. Nothing more."

"You wanted to see us, Yer Lordship," Amown spoke up.

Herod glanced at the dwarf. His smile slipped off his lips as he studied the short fellow. "I did. If you cannot keep the path open then you are of no use to me."

Amown frowned. "It wasn't any of our doing-"

"You are not paid to make excuses for failure," Herod scolded him.

"We're barely paid at all. . ." Amown mumbled.

Herod's eyebrows crashed down. "Speak clearly, or not at all."

Amown bowed his head to hide most of the ugly glare on his face. "Yes, Yer Lordship."

"Have your people relieve my men and clear the remaining rocks. I want that path open before sunset tomorrow," Herod ordered him.

Amown straightened and looked Herod in the eyes. "That can't be done, Yer Lordship, and ya know why not."

Herod's expression darkened. "If your people will not obey by my orders than they shall obey the fires that will lick at their heels as I scatter them before my flame. Do you understand?"

"Aye, Yer Lordship," Amown grudgingly replied. He turned to his fellow dwarves, and the three of them stalked off.

"Follow me," Herod commanded us.

Our dark host led the way through his guards and into the shadowed castle halls. The robed fellow brought up the rear close behind me. I got the feeling of being watched and glanced over my shoulder. He stared straight ahead, but I still had the feeling his eyes were on me, particularly my pocket with the soul stone, rather than the back of his lord's head.

We marched through the gloomy halls with their tiny windows and meager decor. A collection of paintings stood out from the black walls. Most were portraits of men with the same dark expression as Herod, and I could only assume they were ancestors.

Others were quite large, as long and tall as a horse, and showed scenes of violent battle. Dragons flew over a field soaked with the blood of countless fallen men who lay across the plain. A stone castle surrounded by a small village stood in the background, and a forest of burnt trees lined the battlefield.

I stopped and peered at one particular point near the village. The bodies of women and children lay at the edge of detail and blurry color

"The painting was drawn from the memory of my forbearer," a voice spoke up. I started back and found Herod close beside me. His eyes were riveted on the painting. "It was he who took the kingdom from the humans and carved a realm from it."

My eyes flickered to the bodies of the innocents. "Did he kill everyone?"

Herod turned and studied me with the same scrutiny he gave the painting. His lips were tightly pursed. "Conquest demands sacrifice. My line has given much for our realm. I as the last of my family understand than better than the ignoble humans ever could."

TRAITORS AMONG DRAGONS

I frowned. "But wasn't your mother a Maiden?"

He sneered and turned away from me. "What is a maternal line to a race of warriors. Now come."

The confrontation left a bad taste in my mouth. Xander slipped up beside me and looked into my eyes. I managed a small smile and a nod. "I'm fine. Let's just get this vacation over with."

We walked up a flight of stairs to the second floor. Herod dropped us off at our respective chambers. Darda and I were to share one while Spiros and Xander got their own.

We slipped into our dreary abode. A large bed took up much of the wall opposite the wood door. A small table and two wicker chairs stood off to one side, and a simple dresser finished off the spartan furnishings. A few narrow windows stood on either side of the bed.

I spun around to face Darda and crossed my arms over my chest. "All right, 'fess up."

She averted my gaze as she set our bag of supplies on the bed. "I do not know what you mean, Miriam."

"Then you won't mind me frisking you just to see how many daggers you're hiding under that cloak," I commented.

Darda opened the bag and drew out some of my hateful dresses. "I assure you I only possess one dagger."

"So why didn't you have that dagger when we were being dragged into the underbelly of Alexandria by those slave traders?" I questioned her.

Darda sighed and looked up from the clothes. "At that time I was not well-versed in the art of dagger self-defense, or self-defense of any type. That instance, and the battle among the ruins in the Viridi Silva, made me realize that if I was to be of any use to you, Miriam, that I needed to learn how to protect you."

I arched an eyebrow. "So you learned how to use a dagger in three weeks?"

A hint of a smile slipped onto her lips. "I had competent teachers."

"Xander?" I guessed.

She bowed her head. "Among others."

I grinned and shook my head. "I didn't know you could be so sneaky, Darda, but I guess I should've known after how you got me out of the castle. So what else can you do?"

"I-" She paused and glanced at the door. Her look was followed by a knock on said entrance.

"Who is it?" I called out.

"It's me, Olivia," came the voice from the other side.

My shoulders sagged. "Come in."

The door opened and Olivia swept into the room. She wore a tight gray dress with a collar that covered most of her neck and frilly cuffs that hid her hands. The lower hem dragged along the floor and forced her to hold the material in her hands when she moved. Her dark hair was tied back in a tight bun that made me cringe and her face was devoid of makeup. In essence, she was the epitome of a stifled woman without luxury and forever gloomy. She fitted that place perfectly.

Behind her came a wizened old creature that I guessed was a woman. She was dressed in a similar fashion to Olivia, but her hair was a shocking white and her face was so wrinkled I had trouble seeing her eyes. She shut the door behind them as Olivia hurried over and grasped my shoulders.

TRAITORS AMONG DRAGONS

She leaned back and studied me with a broad smile that made me uneasy. "It feels like forever since I last saw you in the courtyard of that other castle! You know, when we were being packed up like luggage."

I slapped a smile on my face and nodded. "Yeah, that was pretty awkward."

Olivia wrapped her arms around herself and paced the floor near the foot of the bed. "God, what an awful time that was! Being picked like cattle and then being stranded out here-" she paused and gestured to the room, "-with that stupid man. And I thought the guys in our world were evil." She spun around and faced me. "Are all the dragon guys like mine, or was I picked with a guy I didn't deserve?"

I bit my tongue to hold back a comment about their like personalities. "I don't think my dragon guy's all that bad."

Her eyes swept over me and a coy smile slipped onto her lips. "If I didn't know any better, I'd say you actually like your slave driver."

I shrugged. "I don't know about-"

"Don't lie," Olivia scolded me as she swept past me and over to the bed. She picked up one of the fine dresses Darda had laid out and admired the material. A soft sigh escaped her lips. "I can see why you liked him. He has better taste in clothes than the one I got stuck with." She turned to face me and gestured down to her bleak attire. "I mean, just look at me. I look like I just got back from my own funeral, and this is what he makes me wear *every day.*"

"It looks-well, warm," I commented.

She expression darkened, and she tossed my dress back on the bed. "In this cold place, and with that dragon? He's so-"

"My Lady," the wizened old woman spoke up.

Olivia glared at her, but shrugged. "But I guess I'm stuck with him." She paused and looked me over with a sly smile. "That is, unless you wouldn't mind trading places with me for a little while, would you? Or maybe sharing your dragon?"

I held up my hands and shook my head. "I don't really think it works that way. Besides, Herod doesn't seem like the kind of guy I'd want to make mad."

She snorted and plopped herself into a nearby wicker chair. "It's hard to tell with him. He only talks to me when he wants to point out that I'm holding my spoon wrong or that I need to talk fancier like everyone seems to do around here."

I wandered over to one of the windows and glanced out. "Maybe he could-" I frowned and turned back to my 'guest.' "Doesn't this look out on the back of the castle?"

Olivia grinned as she stood and strolled over to stand beside me. Her eyes looked out over the view of a courtyard that was a perfect replica of the front one but for the large amount of greenery that made up a well-established garden and orchard. "Stupid, isn't it? The dragons built this castle so they could defend the front and back, so they're mirror images of each other." She nodded at the mountains beyond the valley and a narrow gap in the peaks. "That's where the Coven Caves are. A bunch of witches-"

"My Lady, we are expected at dinner," the old woman reminded her. "And you are

Olivia rolled her eyes, but turned away from the window. "Great. Another hour of silence with Mr. Gloom." Olivia slipped up beside me and looped her arms through one of mine. "But at least I have you for some company. You're going to have to tell me what it's like in the rest of the world. Herod won't even let me leave the castle to climb one of those gnarled old trees."

Olivia's servant opened the door and with Olivia at my side I stumbled into the hall. "You should be more careful," she scolded me as she half-dragged me down the hall.

This was going to be a long adventure.

CHAPTER 6

Olivia clung to my arm like a drowning person to a raft. We descended the stairs and went to the west wing where there was a long, narrow dining hall. An archway led into the room.

Olivia tugged on my arm before we reached the doorway. She glanced over her shoulder at the old woman. Her teeth bit her lower lip before her eyes flickered to me. Her voice was so low I barely caught the words. "Miriam, can I-could I talk to you after dinner? It's really important."

I raised an eyebrow, but nodded. "Sure. What about?"

She shook her head. "Not here, but believe me when I say it could be a matter of life or death."

"My Lady," the old woman spoke up.

Olivia glared at her. "We're going."

TRAITORS AMONG DRAGONS

We continued on our way into the dining hall. The walls were close to the backs of the chairs and with the seats pulled out servants could barely pass. The ceiling was low and the tablecloth over the heavy table was plain and black.

A few narrow windows with colored glass looked out over the dark landscape. The skies were black with thick clouds and a far-off rumble warned of an impending storm.

The only chair with some space and color was the one at the head. There was ample room on three sides for servants to pass, and the high-backed seat was draped in a black cloth with a jagged, scarlet-colored stripe down the center. Naturally, the most dour of us sat in the tall chair. Herod's dark eyes watched everyone who entered through the double doors. They were the only means of accessing the room unless you were as skinny as a bow.

Xander was seated on Herod's left and Spiros was two seats down from him with an empty chair between them. The robe-clad gentleman sat in a short chair behind Herod's seat with a small, round table beside him. There were no utensils or plates, but there was a small cup. Olivia dragged me around the table to the chair beside hers which was situated on Herod's right.

I took my seat with Darda behind me and looked around our company. There was no plate in front of me, but there was a place set in the empty chair opposite mine. "Should I move?"

"No, but the plate should," Olivia replied.

Herod picked up his cup with his left hand and his eyes flickered to me. "My guests are to be on my left side."

Olivia grasped my arm and glared at him. "She's my guest, too." Herod narrowed his eyes and tightened his grip on the neck of the cup.

Xander leaned toward our host and gestured to Olivia and me. "Perhaps we might please the ladies, at least for this evening."

Our host leaned back and set his eyes on Olivia. A sly smile slipped onto his pale lips as he raised his glass. "Then we will have a toast to the ladies, for it is because of one that I have invited you here."

Xander took his cup in hand and furrowed his brow. "I do not understand-"

"I have summoned you here to witness the union of our hearts."

Spiros started back and Xander frowned. "Is that wise, Lord Herod? To create a union so soon after taking your Maiden?"

Olivia blinked at Herod. "You're going to do what with me?"

He grinned and raised his cup to her. "We are to be joined for all eternity, Maiden, and as our tradition demands I have brought guests to bear witness."

She frowned. "What the hell is that supposed to mean?"

"It means our hearts will be as one and our lives will be inextricably intertwined," he told her.

Her mouth dropped open. She pointed to herself and then to him. "That means I'm stuck with you?"

He teased the mouth of his cup against his lips as his sly eyes danced with glee. "Until my dying day."

Olivia's eyebrows crashed down. She leapt to her feet and slammed her hands down on the table. "I refuse!"

Herod lowered his cup and frowned at her. "Seat yourself."

"I'm not going to go through with it!" she insisted.

TRAITORS AMONG DRAGONS

Xander leaned toward our host. "Lord Herod, the joining of the hearts is not to be performed with one unwilling-" Herod waved him away with one hand.

"I need no advice from you, Lord Xander. As for one unwilling, the ceremony does not need either party to be willing, only capable. Her body is strong. She will survive the joining."

Olivia's face turned an unhealthy shade of road rage. "I said I'm not-"

"Seat yourself!" Herod boomed.

The color drained from Olivia's face. All around the table grew quiet. She dropped back into her chair. I could see her shoulders quiver.

That's when it came. The sound was low at first, like a soft whisper in a dark alley. Then it grew louder. The garbled noise morphed into a long, piercing scream. The blood-curdling sound seemed to come from everywhere as it echoed off the walls.

The hairs on the back of my neck stood on end. The soul stone in my pocket burned against my skin. I clapped my hands over my ears to block out the noise, but it rang in my head like a horrible toll of midnight.

Herod slammed his cup onto the table and leapt to his feet. He whipped his head around to face the sorcerer. "Why have you not found the source of that noise?"

The sorcerer met his master's gaze without blinking. "Destiny cannot be found. It must be met."

Our host's face lost much of its color. His hands at his sides shook, but he balled them into steady fists. "There is no destiny to these wailings. They are nothing more than a ruse to strike me at a moment of weakness, but I shall not be weak." He lifted his gaze to the ceiling and raised his voice. "I shall not!"

"Then you have nothing to fear, My Lord," the sorcerer replied.

The noise stopped. Everyone but the sorcerer looked around the room as though anticipating another attack. Nothing happened.

Herod half-collapsed into his seat. He grabbed his cup with a shaking hand and took a heavy dose of his drink. "I have made my decision. The ceremony will take place this night an hour after this meal,." His steady gaze turned to Xander. "If you do not wish to attend then I will have to ask you to leave."

Xander frowned. "The trail is hardly passable after the landslide, and a storm threatens the entire mountain."

Herod leaned back in his high-backed seat and swished around the contents of his cup. "What is that to me? That is-" he paused and his eyes flickered to Xander, "-unless you agree to be my witnesses for the ceremony. If you do I will overlook a minor detail of which my sorcerer has informed me."

Xander arched an eyebrow. "And what might that detail be, Lord Herod?"

Herod's gaze swept over our company. He paused on me. The warm soul stone shifted in my pocket. Herod turned his gaze to Xander and smiled. "That you have brought with you a very great treasure. One that is considered priceless among our race."

Xander managed to smile. "Lord Herod, I have never been adept with riddles. Please speak-"

"I speak of the sword."

TRAITORS AMONG DRAGONS

I straightened and blinked at our dark host. Xander closed his eyes and bowed his head. "Your sorcerer has good senses, Lord Herod. I have brought with me the sword of my ancestors, Bucephalus."

Herod leaned toward Xander and eyed him without blinking. "I would like to examine this sword, as a favor to your host."

Xander pursed his lips, but glanced at Spiros. His captain stood and unsheathed his sword. Out of the sheath came the blue-tinged blade of Bucephalus. Spiros handed the blade to Xander, who offered the weapon to our host.

Herod took the weapon in hand and studied the blade. He took one of the small table knives and dragged the sharp point against the weapon. The knife didn't even leave a scuff in the blade. "Stunning." His gaze flickered to Xander. "Have you deciphered how your ancestors made such a strong blade out of such weak material?"

Xander shook his head. "No, but the world is not what it used to be. Such weapons are of little use in this current age."

One corner of Herod's lips twitched upward before he returned the sword to Xander. "You think very highly of this age of ours, Lord Xander, for one who hid a precious item on one's servant."

Spiros handed the sheath to Xander who slipped the blade into its home and clasped the belt around his own waist. "A mere precaution against thieves, Lord Herod. The sword is very valuable if only for its great age."

Herod studied Xander with his sly eyes. "Under the circumstances, Lord Xander, I must insist your weapon be placed in my custody. I cannot trust one who harbors such weapons in my home without my knowledge. That is-" he leaned toward Xander, "-unless you wish to oblige me my simple request."

My dragon lord pursed his lips together, but bowed his head. "We will attend."

"Excellent!" Herod answered. The look of triumph in his eyes made me cringe. "I could not have found a more worthy name to affix to the witness document. Now-" He glanced at Olivia and frowned. "Where is the necklace I asked you to wear this evening?"

Olivia turned her face away and shrugged. "I don't know. Judith put it somewhere and can't remember where that was. I think she's going crazy in her old age." I noticed the woman behind her tense and press her lips tightly together.

Herod's eyes flickered to the servant woman. "If that is true then she will be duly punished."

Olivia whipped her head back to him and frowned. "What's that supposed to mean? Are you calling me a-"

"Calm yourself, Maiden. Anger creates wrinkles," he scolded her.

"I have a name!" she growled.

"And one day you may have enough of my respect that I would use it, but this night is not that day," he returned. He clapped his hands together. A procession of servants entered the room, each carrying a platter of food. "Now we will eat and prepare for the ceremony."

The platters were set before us as Olivia tilted her chin up and looked down her nose at her dragon lord. "What if I refuse to go through with it?" she challenged him.

He looked straight into her eyes as he stabbed a hunk of meat. A hush fell over the room. Servants paused mid-serve. Olivia's quivering eyes flickered from the meat to the pale face of Herod. A sly smile curled onto his lips.

"If you refuse the next wail from a woman shall be your own. Do you understand?" She swallowed the lump in her throat and nodded. Herod dropped the hunk of meat onto his plate and leaned back. "Good. Then let us dine."

CHAPTER 7

The last half of the meal was as uneventful as the first half was eventful. We were wined and dined by our dark host, and I was never so glad to leave as when we stood from that table. Olivia hadn't said a single word after her last outburst. Her sullen eyes glared one last time at our host before we were marched single-file out of the narrow room.

Out in the hallway Xander set his hand on the small of my back and leaned toward me. "May I escort you to your room, my Maiden?"

I arched an eyebrow, but something in his voice told me that would be a good idea. "Sure. Just lead the way."

Xander, with Darda and Spiros behind us, escorted me up to my room and opened the door. I stepped in, but Xander paused in the doorway and turned to our friends.

TRAITORS AMONG DRAGONS

"Spiros, remain at the door. Darda, if you would please fetch your lady a platter of meat."

"But I'm not-" There was that look again. I glanced at Darda and smiled. "If you would."

Darda bowed her head. "If it pleases My Lady." She turned and left us.

Xander stepped inside and shut the door behind us. I walked over to the bed and spun around to face Xander before I folded my arms over my chest. "What was all that about?"

Xander tilted his head toward the door and pressed a finger to his lips. "Not so loud."

I raised an eyebrow. "Do the walls have ears?"

He swept his eyes over the room. "Perhaps, and caution is the best practice."

I leaned my back against one of the posts on my bed and lowered my voice. "So mind bringing me up to speed about that dinner?"

"Do you refer to the ceremony, or the sound we heard during dinner?" he asked me.

"Both, but let's start with the hair-raising scream."

My dragon lord pursed his lips. "It is called the Cry of the Traitor, and for those of Herod's house it is an omen of death."

I tilted my head to one side and furrowed my brow. "So why is it called the Cry of the Traitor?"

"Long ago the black dragons were betrayed by one of their Maidens," he told me as he walked over to stand before me. "The Maiden was put to death for her treachery, but her spirit returns to warn the lords of their impeding death."

I wrapped my arms around myself and shuddered. "So is this a three-screams, he's out kind of thing?"

"The scream ebbs and flows in its own time, and grows increasingly louder until the time of death, at which point the sound ceases and the lord is dead."

I cringed. "No wonder Herod's so high-strung."

He nodded. "Yes, and I see now why Herod's men greeted us on the path and not the dwarves. Amown's people would not venture forth under such auspices noises."

I shrugged. "Why not? It's not for them."

Xander shook his head. "The death has not always been of the lord alone. War and plague have also proceeded the cry."

I swept my eyes over the room. "So is it safe for us to be here?"

Xander walk over to one of the windows near the bed and looked out. A flash of lightning was followed shortly by a bellowing boom of thunder. The hard patter of rain beat against the glass. "Unfortunately, we have no choice. The storm keeps us prisoners, as does my promise for us to attend the ceremony."

I plopped myself onto the side of my bed close to where Xander stood. "So what's this ceremony so important that we get to spend a stormy night in a haunted castle?"

Xander leaned an arm against the side of the windowsill and looked out on the bleak landscape. "The Joining of the Hearts is where a dragon grants a human their long life. It is a transfer of the dragon's heart, and some say their soul, into the body of the human."

"You mean like what Darda did with her husband?" I guessed.

He dropped his arm to his side and turned to me. "The ceremony is the same, but the reasons are quite different."

TRAITORS AMONG DRAGONS

I arched an eyebrow. "So how come you and I haven't done it?"

"Because I care too much for you."

I blinked at him. "So you care so much for me that you won't let me live as long as you?" A funny thought entered my mind. I leaned toward him and stuck my chin out as I squinted. "You're not keeping me from having those wings so I have to be in your arms, are you?"

Xander strode over and took a seat beside me. He clasped our hands together and studied mine as he turned them over in his fingers. A funeral couldn't have dropped my face faster than his sad, searching eyes. "The ceremony is very dangerous. If performed incorrectly, one or both parties might die."

I winced. "And that lone party is usually the human, isn't it?"

He raised his eyes to mine and nodded. "Yes. The human body has the chance to reject the heart and the exertion of the refusal destroys them. I could not risk your life, nor would I wish to perform the ceremony against your will as Herod is doing to his Maiden."

I smiled and shrugged. "Maybe all this mountain-climbing and avalanche dodging will make me stronger." Another boom outside reminded me of the dreary atmosphere around us. "So besides the storm raging outside and Herod's threat to do away with us in some horrible, unknown way, why do we have to be here for this ceremony?"

"In previous times humans and dragons lied about their connections to gain pardons or influence. Two witnesses were then required to sign a document stating to the authenticity of the union," he explained.

I furrowed my brow. "Can they prove that someone's joined to somebody else?"

He nodded. "Yes. Those who are joined and are physically close to one another will feel the other's physical pain. One need only hide them from one another and prick a certain spot on the body-"

"-and ask the other person where that spot was," I finished for him.

He smiled. "Your wit never ceases to amaze me."

I swept my eyes over the dark room. "Flattery will get you a lot of places, but not in this creepy joint. Anyway, what if everybody-the signers and the people who said they were joined-were caught lying about that? What would happen to them?"

"They would all be put to death by their beating hearts being cut from their chests."

I cringed and clutched my chest over my heart. "Ouch. That's a really Draconian way of dealing with that."

Xander released my hands and stood so he faced me. "The punishment is necessary in order to ensure the integrity of the joining."

I raised an eyebrow. "You're not going to try to drop me into a forest against if I disagree with another tradition, are you?"

He smiled and shook his head. "No."

"Good. I'm glad you agree with-"

"For one, the nearest forest is in another valley."

My face fell and I narrowed my eyes at him. "Very funny."

He bowed low to me. "Always at your service, my Maiden."

TRAITORS AMONG DRAGONS

I winced. "Could you not call me that? It reminds me of the way Herod says it to Olivia."

Xander knelt in front of me and settled his hands on my lap as he looked into my eyes. "Know that I will never be to you as Herod is to his Maiden."

I smiled at him and squeezed his hands. "I know." Another flash of lightning lit up the room. I scooted a little closer to him and glanced over my shoulder at the dark window. "You wouldn't mind staying with me until the ceremony, would you? It's not that I'm scared or anything, it's just if I'm going to be frightened out of my wits I'm going to want you to keep me from hurting myself."

He slipped onto the bed and wrapped his arm around my waist. "It would be my pleasure."

I leaned the side of my head against his shoulder and sighed. My eyes flickered up to his face. There was a tension in his look that made me lift my head. "What *else* is wrong?"

He looked down at the sword that was between us. "Herod's sorcerer-"

"The one Amown called Mordecai?" I asked him.

He nodded. "Yes, the gentleman behind Herod's seat during dinner. It is most curious that he did not inform Herod of the trouble at the arch."

"Maybe Herod didn't care," I suggested.

Xander shook his head. "Herod keeps a firm grasp on those who enter his realm, as we witnessed with the sword."

I nodded. "Yeah. For a second there I thought he was going to keep it."

My dragon lord slipped the sword into his lap and pursed his lips as he studied the simple sheath. "As did I, and he would have kept you under closer watch if he had known about your heritage."

I arched an eyebrow. "Why? I don't know how to do what I've done."

"But you still present an uncontrolled risk, and for that he would see you as a threat," he pointed out.

I looked at the floor and furrowed my brow. "There's something else. That Mordecai guy was watching me as we walked to the castle. I swore he was looking at my pocket, the one with my soul stone."

Xander replaced his sword at his side. "How very unusual. Herod would have certainly confiscated such a prize if he had known of its existence."

"I know they're rare, but are they dangerous?" I asked him.

He nodded. "They can be used as weapons if that is the power that was granted to them."

There came a knock on the door. Xander glanced at the entrance. "Yes?"

"My Lord," came Spiros's call. "The ceremony is about to begin."

Xander stood and helped me to my feet. "We are coming."

"Ready or not. . ." I muttered.

CHAPTER 8

We left the room and found a pair of guards ready to escort us.

I didn't fail to notice a missing party and looked to Xander. "What about Darda?"

"She will be fine," he assured me.

We were escorted down the hall to the opposite end of the castle from the cramped dining room. A long, wide room was presented to us. The left wall held windows that looked out on the dark, stormy night. At the far end of the space was a throne carved from the dragon-blackened stone. A narrow carpet of red led from the pair of doors up to the throne.

A small crowd of servants stood off to one side and in front of the throne. Their sullen faces dulled the dreary atmosphere of the room with a heavy cloud of morbidity. They watched us with lifeless eyes as we approached them.

I leaned toward Xander and lowered my voice to a whisper. "Herod's not exactly popular with his servants, is he?"

Xander shook his head. "I fear not. Many are humans who were purchased on the slave market."

I frowned. "And he keeps them as slaves?"

"Unfortunately, yes."

I huddled closer to my kind dragon lord as we were led to the opposite side of the rug from the sullen servants. The guards took up positions on either side of the throne. The door to the throne room opened, and we turned to see Herod enter. Behind him came Mordecai, but no Olivia. Mordecai took a place in front of the throne and faced the congregation while Herod stood off to one side. It wasn't the one with the servants.

He swept his dark eyes over the room and frowned before he looked to the guards on either side of the throne. "Where is my Maiden?"

The doors once again creaked open, and the wizened old woman from before shuffled inside. She walked up to Herod and bowed her head low to him. "I am sorry, My Master, but My Lady is delayed with her dress. If My Master would oblige her with only a few more minutes-"

Herod's expression darkened. "Bring her here at once, or you will both suffer the-" A figure stepped into the room.

All eyes fell on the newcomer. The feminine form of Olivia was drenched in a thick layer of black cloth. Her funeral attire stretched from below her chin and dragged on the floor behind her in a long train. Olivia's hands were enveloped in frilly black lace that covered all but the tips of her fingernails. Her facial features were distorted by the long, thick veil covered her front and trailed down her back to her waist.

Olivia stopped just inside the doorway. The old woman shuffled over and took her arm. She led the funeral bride down the aisle to stand in front of the throne and facing Mordecai. Herod moved so they stood shoulder-to-shoulder. His narrowed eyes flickered to her obscured face.

"Shall I begin?" Mordecai asked him.

Herod pursed his lips, but nodded. Mordecai stepped up to Herod and held up his hands so the palms were even with the dragon's shirt. A faint blue light pulsed from his palms and connected to form a single band. The band of light floated forward and penetrated Herod's chest. The dragon lord grunted and clenched his teeth.

Xander stiffened beside me. I looked up into his face and saw that his eyes were riveted on Mordecai's hands.

The beam of light receded from Herod's chest, taking with it a glob of red. The red pulsed with the consistency of a heartbeat. Herod stumbled to one side, but one of the guards beside the throne caught and steadied him.

Mordecai kept his arms rigid as he stepped to one side to stand before Olivia. The beam slowly penetrated her chest. A deep, stifled gasp emanated from beneath the veil and she doubled over as the red heart pushed inside her. Mordecai clasped his hands together and extinguished the blue light.

Olivia's legs collapsed beneath her and she dropped to her knees. The other guard rushed to her side and grabbed her arm. A terrible groan passed from Olivia's lips and her whole body shook.

Herod pushed his guard away and knelt beside Olivia. He grabbed the veil and tore it from her face, revealing Olivia's pale, sweat-soaked face. Her eyes were devoid of expression as her body twitched and squirmed. Every jerky movement made her gasp and groan.

Herod looked up at Mordecai. "What is the matter with her?"

The sorcerer tilted his head to one side and studied the young woman. "Her body is having trouble absorbing the heart."

Herod sneered at his Maiden and stood before he tossed the veil away. The flimsy cloth fluttered into Olivia's lap. "Pathetic."

The old woman shuffled up to them and knelt in front of Olivia. "What would My Master wish to do with My Lady?"

The dragon lord turned his back on them. "Remove her from my sight."

"And if she were to die?" Judith asked him.

He lifted his chin and glared at the top of the tall throne. "Then do with her as you see fit."

Judith pursed her wrinkled lips, but nodded. With the help of the guard, she assisted Olivia to her feet. They stumbled down the aisle past us. Unbidden tears slipped from my eyes as I glimpsed Olivia's ashen face. Her empty eyes stared unblinkingly at the ground.

They moved on without stopping and left the room. The servants quickly and quietly followed. Silence reigned but for the thundering storm outside.

I swallowed the lump in my throat and slipped my hand into Xander's. He looked down at me, and I quietly mouthed the word 'please.' Xander glanced back at Herod. The man's back was turned to us. "Lord Herod-" Herod shook himself and turned to us.

"Yes, the document." He looked to Mordecai, who gestured to a parchment and quill pen on a table beside the throne. Herod looked to one side and waved his hand at the document. "Sign it and begone."

Xander grasped my hand and led me over to the table with him in the lead. Mordecai lifted the pen and held it out to me as I stood partially behind Xander. I wrapped my fingers around the quill, but when I tried to pull it free found he had a tight grip. I looked into his face. His blue eyes stared back and searched mine.

I frowned. "What?"

Mordecai released the pen and bowed his head as he stepped back. "It is nothing."

I studied him for a second before I bent down and scribbled my name on a line. There was a brief interruption when, out of the corner of my eye, I watched Herod stiffen for a moment. He spun around and stalked down the hall with the guard close at his heels.

I straightened and looked at Xander. He took the pen and scribbled his name on the parchment. He handed the pen back to Mordecai, and with our duty performed we strode from the throne room. My dragon lord directed me into my bedroom and, with Spiros once more at the watch, shut the door behind us.

Xander turned to me with a downcast expression. "I am sorry you were a witness to the worst of my race."

I turned my back on him and wrapped my arms around me. A crooked, humorless smile slipped onto my lips. "It's fine. You guys can't all be nice, right? Otherwise I wouldn't feel so bad for the humans that are left."

Xander walked up to me and grasped my upper arms. His voice was low and soft. "You have seen much of my world-" I turned to face him and shook my head.

"Don't give me the spiel about how it's a nice place full of good people. I know it is, and I've seen enough of the ugly to know it's no better nor worse than mine," I told him.

He smiled. "Actually, I was about to tell you the shark-finned people of Reef Bay are far worse. They eat their wives."

I leaned back and eyed his face. "Seriously?"

Xander leaned down and pecked a kiss on my lips. "No, but I find the idea very amusing."

I rolled my eyes and pushed him away. "Only because you wouldn't be the one being turned into fish food."

He chuckled. "If you taste half as delightful as your scent than I would be most pleased to have a bite of you myself."

I spun him around and pointed at the door. "Out." There came another knock on my door. "Nobody's home!"

"Miriam," came Darda's scolding voice.

"Enter," Xander called out.

Darda slipped inside with the promised platter of meat. I nodded at the food. "You're too late. I lost my appetite."

"Do you bring more than food?" Xander asked her as she set the platter on the small table.

Darda turned to us and nodded. "Yes, My Lord. The servants are all aflutter with the Cry that comes most every night and grows louder around their lord."

"Is Herod in good health?" he asked her.

She gave a nod. "He is, My Lord, but his appetite is none too good with the Cry bothering him, and just as I was leaving the kitchen I a pair of the liverymen come inside. It seems Lord Herod called for his horse some ten minutes ago and rode off in the direction of the Coven Caves."

Xander arched an eyebrow. "Alone?"

She nodded. "Yes, My Lord. Even his sorcerer was left behind."

Xander pursed his lips and paced the room with his chin cupped in one hand. "How very unusual."

"Why? Doesn't he always like to go riding alone in the middle of a storm with a crying ghost calling his doom?" I quipped.

My dragon lord stopped and looked to me. "Herod keeps a very delicate balance of power over these mountains. The dwarves are paid for their loyalty-"

"But not enough," I reminded him.

"-and Mordecai is used as his protection against the very witches to whom he has traveled alone," he finished.

"So what's at the Coven Caves?" I wondered.

"Witches."

I ran a hand through my hair and sighed. "Witches. Of course." I walked over and plopped myself on the end of my bed. "I'd say ask Herod what he was doing, but he'd probably demand our execution on treason charges."

Xander dropped his arms to his sides and nodded. "Unfortunately, in his fragile state of mind you might not be far off. However, I will make inquiries on the morrow. For now the hour is late, and I am sure you wish for some rest."

CHAPTER 9

The next few hours were long and frustrating. I tossed and turned. The bed was hard, the sheets rough, the room was cold, and I just couldn't get Olivia's pale face out of my mind. The ceremony had been like watching a funeral, but where the dead person had been buried alive. I sat up and glanced over the room. The noise of the storm had receded, but a few faint drops of rain pattered against the narrow windows.

Darda sat up from where she lay on the floor beside my bed. "Can you not sleep?"

I tossed aside the covers and swung my legs over the other side of the bed. "No. I guess I'm just not used to this place."

"Would you care for a glass of warm milk? Or perhaps some of the meat I brought?" she suggested.

TRAITORS AMONG DRAGONS

I smiled, but shook my head. "No. I think I'll take a walk. Maybe the exercise will make me sleepy."

Darda stood and grabbed our cloaks from the table. She wore a long, thick nightgown that looked like it came from Lumberjacks Unlimited than the Victoria's Secret catalog. I couldn't laugh, though. I wore the same thing. "Then allow me to accompany you."

I took my cloak from her and smiled. "Thanks. If we meet any ninjas you can fend them off."

She arched an eyebrow. "'Ninjas?'"

I sighed as I shrugged into my cloak. "I'll explain it to you on the walk."

We slipped out of the room and into the black halls. The torches that lit the passages still crackled with fire as we crept down the stairs and turned left toward the rear of the castle. We emerged into the cool, damp air of the dark garden courtyard. I took a deep breath of fresh air after the dank, dry atmosphere of the gloomy castle. My nostrils smelled the fragrant flowers and wet leaves of the tall, broad-leafed arbors that resembled fruit trees. A gravel path wound its way beneath their canopies, and every now and again there were stone benches placed near the trunks.

I leaned toward Darda and lowered my voice to a whisper. "I can't believe Herod has something like this in his castle."

"Nor can I," she agreed.

I looked down the gravel path. The trail wound so sharply around bunches of tall bushes that I couldn't see what lay beyond the corner. I looked to my companion and grinned. "What say we go exploring?"

She pursed her lips. "I do not believe that would be wise, Miriam. Herod is a very suspicious man, and if he were to see us-" I wrinkled my nose and waved my hand at her.

"He's probably still trying to divine his future with those witches," I told her. I grabbed her hand and gave her a tug. "Besides, we're only walking here. What's the worst that could happen?"

I pulled the reluctant Darda to my side and we strolled along the gravel path. The pitter patter of rain on the leaves took me away from the horrible black stones that encased the wondrous garden. It reminded me of rainy days in my apartment when I was grateful for a warm cup of cocoa and a hot blanket. I couldn't help but sigh at the memories of those halcyon days of boredom and relaxation.

My reminisces were interrupted by the terrible Cry of the Traitor. Its penetrating wail seemed to come from everywhere and nowhere. Darda and I stopped in our tracks and clapped our hands over our ears to block the piercing yell, but to no avail. The sound sank into our bodies like an earthquake and rattled our bones.

A loud, shrieking voice cut through the wailing. "Maiden!"

A shadow stumbled around the corner. The stooped figure ambled toward us and I glimpsed the shining black eyes of the dark dragon lord, Herod. He was like a drunk man possessed as he rushed toward us.

The color drain from my face as I stepped in front of Darda. My hands were still over my ears, and I had to raise my voice to hear myself over the horrible crying. "I-I'm really sorry! I didn't know this place was off-"

TRAITORS AMONG DRAGONS

The black lord reached me and grabbed my arms in his iron grip. He looked into my eyes with such hatred that I felt my flesh burn. "Maiden! Maiden! Treacherous Delilah!"

Herod dipped his head and coughed. A splattering of blood and clay spilled onto the gravel and me. He looked up at me one last time before his eyes rolled back and his head drooped to one side. The terrible wailing stopped at the same time, but left our bodies ringing with its echoes.

But I didn't have time to think about that as Herod fell face-first against me and went limp. I slipped my arms under his and stumbled back beneath his greater weight. Our chests were pressed against one another. My heart beat, but there was no like echo from his chest.

A voice in my head told me to scream, and I did, good and loud. I also yanked my arms away and stumbled back, sending the lord's cooling body toppling face-first into the gravel. Darda caught me as I tripped over my own frightened feet.

Other pairs of feet pounded onto the small patio of stones behind us. A contingent of guards looked out on the horrible scene of their lord lying face-down in the gravel. They rushed over and surrounded us.

The leader, the same man from the head of the trail, knelt beside Herod and turned him over. Herod's face was a twisted mess of agony and anger, frozen in place by his sudden and painful death. His eyes stared unblinkingly at the falling rain. "Lord Herod!" The guard looked up at Darda and me. "What happened?"

I shook my head. "I-I don't know. He just came around the corner screaming about Maidens and fell against me."

The guard's eyes narrowed at us. He set his lord's body on the ground and stood. "What was it he was screaming?"

The other soldiers surrounded and moved in closer to us. Darda stiffened and I felt her hand dip into her cloak, but I held her arm and swallowed my rising fear. "He said something about Maidens, and a name. I think it was Deli-something."

The leader unsheathed his weapon and hissed out a single word: "Delilah." The other soldiers followed suit.

My eyes flickered from one blade to another. "Hold on a second. We didn't do anything. I don't know why he said that."

"He spoke the name of a traitor," a voice interrupted the suffocating mood.

The leader of the soldiers glanced at the entrance to the garden and my eyes followed suit. Mordecai strolled over to us with his hands clasped behind his back. He wore his normal robed outfit with the strange red cloth around his neck.

The soldiers parted and the sorcerer stopped beside beside Herod. He knelt down and closed Herod's eyes. Mordecai hovered his hand down Herod's stiff face and drew it down the body to the mess of blood and mud on the man's chest. He looked up at Darda and me. "What brought you to the garden?"

"I wanted some fresh air," I told him. I nodded at Darda. "She didn't have anything to do with this. It was all my idea. I didn't know Herod get so mad he'd have a heart attack about it."

Mordecai stood and his eyes flickered to the lead guard. "When did your lord return?"

TRAITORS AMONG DRAGONS

"Only ten minutes ago," the guard replied. His hard eyes glanced at Darda and me. "Hardly time for poisoning."

I bristled at the comment. "We didn't murder him! It was an-"

"This was no accident," Mordecai interrupted as he set his eyes on me. "A dust of magic covers him."

"Maybe he got it from the caves," I suggested.

Mordecai arched an eyebrow. "How did you learn he went to the caves?"

The guard clenched his teeth and stepped closer to me with his blade at the ready. "The sorcerer is right. Neither of us mentioned where he-" A terrible wail came from the castle tower.

I thought it was the Cry of the Traitor returned for more victims, but Judith stumbled into the garden. Her wild eyes fell on us and she rushed over to our large group. She pawed at the lead guard's chest plate. "Lord Blastus! It is My Lady! She's...she's dead!"

Mordecai pursed his lips. "Where is she?"

Judith pointed at one of the tower windows above the gardens. "In her room!"

Mordecai turned to the group of guards. "Half of you remain with the fallen lord. The rest of you will me, and bring them-" he nodded at Darda and me, "-with you." Two of the guards grabbed our arms.

I thrashed in their grasp. "Knock it off! We didn't do anything!"

Judith's wild gaze fell on me. Her lips curled into an ugly snarl as her eyes narrowed. She lunged forward and clawed at me with her shriveled hands. The orange-ish powder that covered her fingers and palms dusted onto me and tickled my nose even as she tried to scratch it off. The

67

guard who held me turned to one side and took most of the cutting. "You killed her! You killed them all!"

"Hold her still!" Mordecai ordered as he swept past her.

"Who are you to give orders?" Blastus spoke up.

Mordecai paused a few feet from us and half-turned to our group. "Would your orders be any different?"

Blastus nodded at Darda and me. "Yes. They shall be placed in the dungeon."

"I will not allow that."

My heart beat quickened as I recognized the voice of my dragon lord. He and Spiros entered the garden, completing the chaos that now engulfed the entire castle. All the windows were alight and people leaned out to see what was the matter.

Xander marched toward us with Bucephalus at his hip. The unoccupied guards stepped into his path, including Blastus. Xander looked past them at Mordecai and us. "What is the meaning of this? Where is Lord Herod?"

"Our lord is dead," Blastus informed him.

"And he thinks we did it!" I chimed in.

Xander narrowed his eyes. "I will take custody of my Maiden."

Mordecai stepped to the front of the group and shook his head. "That cannot be allowed, Lord Xander. She is under suspicion of the murder of a dragon lord."

Blastus raised his weapon to Xander. "Or are you a member to this plot?"

Xander swooped back and unsheathed Bucephalus. A swift strike and Blastus's blade was broken into two pieces. The top piece clattered to the gravel ground. The soldiers leapt forward and surrounded Xander and Spiros. Spiros drew his weapon and spun around to guard their rear.

TRAITORS AMONG DRAGONS

Xander's narrowed eyes looked through a pair of soldiers and into Blastus's surprised face. "Your lord cared nothing for his Maiden, but do not underestimate my will to protect mine."

A flash of blue light exploded in the middle of the group. The men lowered their swords and threw up their unguarded arm to cover their eyes. I half-turned away and blinked into the bright light.

Mordecai stepped into the point where the blue light had emerged. He looked from Blastus to Xander. "Noble words, Lord, but foolish at this time. Lord Herod is dead, and someone is responsible."

"What about My Lady?" Judith shrieked.

Mordecai gestured to Judith. "The Maiden's condition demands our attention, and your Maiden cannot be left alone *for any reason.* Do you understand?"

Xander straightened and sheathed Bucephalus. "I believe I do, but wherever my Maiden goes, I go."

Mordecai glanced at Blastus. "Does that please the high guard of the castle?"

Blastus also tucked his weapon into its sheath and nodded. "It does, for the moment."

"Then let us to the Maiden's room."

CHAPTER 10

Half the guards remained in the garden to remove Herod's corpse while Mordecai with Judith at his side led our group into the castle. We hurried up the stairs to the third floor and into one of the chambers. The door was open, and inside we found Olivia on the bed. She lay at an angle across the bed and her pale face was distorted by the same agony as that of Herod. Her empty eyes stared up at the ceiling.

Mordecai turned to Judith. "Were you here when the attack struck her?"

Judith shook her head. "I-I left her to fetch some food, and when I came back I heard her cry out. She was writhing in pain, and then she. . .she-" She cupped her face in her hands and let out a sob.

TRAITORS AMONG DRAGONS

A pair of the guards straightened Olivia on the bed before they stepped back and Mordecai took their places. He closed her eyes and examined her clothes.

"Can you tell if the Maiden was attacked first and Our Lord suffered the consequences of it as well?" Blastus asked him.

Mordecai dropped his arms to his sides and pursed his lips. "I cannot tell from a cursory examination, but such a suggestion is possible."

"That should rule us out," I spoke up. I nodded at Darda. "Darda and I were in the garden when Herod stumbled up to us. We couldn't have been in two places at once."

Blastus turned to me and scowled. "Unless the Maiden was poisoned. The time for the poison to take effect would have given you ample opportunity to move to the garden."

I squirmed in the hold of the guard and glared at Blastus. "Why the hell would we kill her? Huh?"

He stepped up and towered over me. His hard eyes glared down into mine. "I do not know, but if you are proven to be the assassin then I will personally execute you."

Xander slipped between us and bumped Blastus back with his body. "That must first be proven, though what Miriam spoke is true. We had no reason to kill either of them, but many others could not say the same."

Blastus straightened and set his hand on the hilt of his weapon. "Do you infer that I-"

Mordecai raised his arms above his head and his voice boomed over the arguing. "Enough!" The pair of dragons glared at each other, but were quieted. Mordecai lowered his arms and cleared his throat before he turned to Xander. "Lord Xander, please allow us some time to look into the details of these deaths. In the meanwhile, we must ask that your Maiden and her servant remain in the cells beneath the castle."

Spiros stepped forward. "The rot alone would kill her."

"My companion is correct, the cell is no place for a woman," Xander argued.

"I will make my examinations brief. If you would but give me four hours, I will bring a conclusion to you," Mordecai assured him.

Xander pursed his lips and glanced over his shoulder at me. "Whatever your decision, I will abide by it."

I pursed my lips and glanced to Darda. She nodded. I sighed and turned my attention to Mordecai. "These cells better have a bed."

He smiled and bowed his head. "I assure you they do."

What he didn't assure me was if they were soft which they weren't. The cells lay twenty feet below the ground and were accessed through a side door on the ground floor. There were no windows for ventilation and no other door save the one we passed through as Blastus marched Darda and me into the single long hall. On either side were small five-by-five foot cells carved from the gray rock.

Rusted metal bars gave us peeks into the accommodations. They weren't five-star. Hell, they weren't even five-slum. The walls were dank with water and produced healthy colonies of dark-green mold. The torches that hung between the cells created smoke that had nowhere to escape so the whole place looked like London during a smog epidemic.

Blastus stopped in front of a pair and nodded at the doors. "Place them in separate cells."

TRAITORS AMONG DRAGONS

The doors were unlocked and we stepped inside. I cringed as my door was slammed shut behind me. Xander stepped up to the bars. I turned and smiled at him. "I have one last request before they lead you out of here."

He grasped the bars. "Anything."

"I want a vacation after this mess is over."

He smiled and nodded. "I swear it."

"That is enough. You must leave," Blastus demanded.

Xander let his hands drop to his sides. My pulse quickened as he stepped back. I rushed up to the bars and grabbed one of his hands. Maybe it was the torch smoke, but a couple of annoying tears slipped down my cheeks. "Try to keep out of trouble while I'm in here, okay?"

He reached through the bars and brushed away a loose tear. "You will not remain here long. I promise you that."

"I ordered you to leave," Blastus insisted.

I pursed my lips, but reluctantly pulled my hand free of his grasp. Blastus's men surrounded Spiros and Xander. The former bowed his head to me while the latter didn't take his eyes off me until he could no longer turn his head that far.

Mordecai remained behind a moment longer than the rest. His blue eyes studied me for a moment before he bowed his head. "Goodnight, Maiden."

I turned away and crossed my arms over my chest. His soft footsteps disappeared down the stone hall. My about-face meant I got to see the bed to which he referred earlier.

It was a bench carved from the stone. I lowered myself onto its hard surface and kicked a loose wall shard on the ground. "Stupid dragon lords and their stupid paranoia. . ." I looked down at myself. The top of my dress was still covered in a splattering of blood mixed with clay. "Couldn't they have at least given me time to change?"

"I am sure we will be shortly freed," Darda's voice called from the adjoining cell.

"You might be right, but you might be wrong. Either way, I'm not wearing this stupid thing, at least not most of it." I grabbed the hem of my dress and pulled. The cloth came away with a nice tearing noise, and soon I had

"What are you doing?" Darda asked me.

"Solving at least one problem," I commented as I tossed the lower part of the dress aside. I stretched my legs in front of me and wiggled my toes. "At least now this stupid thing won't trip me."

"But you might catch cold," she pointed out.

"Then I can give it to the guards," I quipped as I shifted atop the furniture. One of the rough points of the 'bed' stabbed into my rear. A quick glare at the hard rock didn't intimidate it. I glanced at the wall to my right. "You don't happen to have an extra pillow in there, do you, Darda?"

"I would be grateful if I had one to give to you."

I sighed as I gingerly lay down on the hard bed. "That's what I thought." My mind wandered back to the scene of the maybe-crime. I frowned and tilted my face toward the wall. "Darda?"

"Yes?"

"Do you know why the guards got mad when I mentioned that name?"

"Yes. It is the name of the Maiden who treacherously murdered her dragon lord."

I shut my eyes and dragged my hand down my face. "Of course it is. . ."

Clink.

I opened my eyes and looked around. Nothing stirred.

Clink.

TRAITORS AMONG DRAGONS

"Darda, could you please stop that tapping."

"But I am not tapping."

I sat up and frowned. "If you're not tapping then what am I hearing?"

I heard Darda shuffle toward the wall and pause. "I hear nothing."

"Lemme see something." I pressed my ear against the bed and closed my eyes.

Clink.

My eyes flew open and I drew my face away from the bed. "It's coming from the wall!"

"Allow me to listen." I resumed my listening and there was another pause from Darda's cell. "You are correct, but perhaps the noise is a guard striking his staff against the floor above us."

A sudden thought drained the color from my face. "You don't suppose there are ghosts down here, do you?"

"Anything is possible in this world."

I sat up and wrapped my arms around myself. "There goes any chance for sleep. . ."

CHAPTER 11

Fate had the same idea. The words had hardly left my mouth when I heard the clomp of footsteps march down the stairs and into the passage.

"Miriam!" Darda whispered.

"Morning already?" I mumbled as I slipped off the bed and shuffled to the cell door. Xander and Mordecai walked toward us with the jailer and his keys ahead of them. There was no sign of anyone else. Their grim faces didn't encourage me as they came up to our cells. "Don't tell me the verdict is in already."

Xander pursed his lips. "Matters have become more complicated." His eyes flickered down to my dress. "What happened?"

TRAITORS AMONG DRAGONS

I raised an eyebrow. "The rats are mean down here, but how can a double-assassination by an unknown assailant or assailants become more complicated?"

The jailer opened my cell and Xander slipped inside to grasp my hands. "Lady Olivia's body has disappeared."

I blinked at him. "Seriously?"

He nodded. "Very seriously."

I looked past him at Mordecai who stood in the passage. "Now do you believe we didn't do it?"

He bowed his head. "I do believe you, but the captain is unconvinced."

"He demands that Darda remain in her cell until Herod's death is solved," Xander added.

My eyes widened as I looked from Mordecai to Xander. "But what if it's never solved?" The men glanced at each other. "Well?"

"I have faith you will solve this mystery," Darda spoke up. I slipped past Xander and hurried to the front of her cell. She stood at the bars with a small smile on her face. "Have you forgotten all those movies you were so kind to relate to me? This is much like them."

I grasped the bars and shook my head. "But those were just movies! I'm not a real detective!"

She lay her hands over mine and shook her head. "You place too little faith on your perseverance, Miriam. I believe that together Lord Xander and you will be able to clear our good names and free me."

My shoulders slumped, but a small smile teased the corners of my lips. "So if this is a mystery what should we call it?"

"Perhaps 'The Dragon and the Detective,'" she suggested.

I snorted. "Sounds good to me."

She looked past me at Xander who came up behind me. "Please be careful, My Lord."

He nodded. "We will. I swear it."

Darda smiled and bowed her head. "Thank you." She returned her attention to me. Her hands fell from mine and she stepped back. "Good luck, Miriam, My Lord. May the gods bless your endeavor and bring with it a swift conclusion."

I pressed my hands against my chest and pursed my lips. "Yeah. Really swift."

Xander set his hands on my shoulders and led me away. Mordecai and the jailer followed. I looked over my shoulder one last time before we left the cell passage. Darda stood near her cell door. She stuck her hand out and waved to me.

I stiffened my upper lip and waved back. "See you soon! And try to keep the mold off you!"

Darda's laugh echoed down the hall. "I will try."

I smiled, and we left the dank cell block and climbed the stairs in the bleak castle. Mordecai guided us down the passage and around a corner where he opened a door. The entrance led into a simple study with a few half-empty bookshelves and a writing desk in the middle.

He swept his hand toward the room. "If you would please enter. I wish to speak with you."

Xander stepped inside and I followed. Mordecai shut the door and moved to stand before us. He clasped his hands behind his back and looked from one of us to the other. I shivered and wrapped my arms around myself.

"May I provide you with a blanket?" Mordecai offered.

I shook my head. "No, but you can exterminate those stupid mice in the dungeon. They sound like they're chipping away at the castle foundation."

His eyebrows crashed down. "No mouse can burrow through the rock upon which this castle stands."

I jerked my thumb over my shoulder. "You'd better tell them that. They're chinking away at it as we speak."

"Of what do you wish to speak with us?" Xander interrupted.

Mordecai bowed his head. "My apologies. I wished to know if you truly intend to find the source of this tragedy."

Xander arched an eyebrow. "Do you suspect the cause was not a mere health defect?"

Mordecai's crafty eyes studied us. "Herod was not well-liked. His enemies list is longer than most, even for a lord of dragons."

"You don't happen to have that list on you, do you?" I spoke up.

He shook his head. "The list would be too long for a roll of parchment to contain. As it stands, if you believe his Maiden and he were felled by the hands of others than you must scour the entirety of the peaks to find the source." His eyes fell on my dress and he paused. His eyebrows shot down as he tilted his head to one side. "Did that blood come from the lord?"

I looked down at myself and nodded. "Yeah. He coughed it out before he collapsed."

Mordecai slipped one of his hands out from behind his back and gestured to the stain. "May I?"

I blinked at him. "May you what?"

A smile played across his lips. "Examine the blood more closely."

I shrugged and puffed out my chest. "Knock yourself out."

Mordecai's eyes flickered to Xander, who nodded. The sorcerer stepped forward and took the cloth in hand. He leaned in close and squinted at the blood spots. "Did he fall before he reached you?"

I shook my head. "I didn't see him fall, but I guess he must have because of the clay."

Xander moved to stand beside Mordecai and in front of me. "Clay?"

I nodded down at my shirt. "Yeah. He got blood and clay on my shirt." I glanced from one face to the other. "Why? Is that important?"

"It might perhaps be," Mordecai replied as he released the front of my dress and turned to Xander. "I would accompany you to the Caves, but I am not welcome there."

I blinked at them. "Where are we going?"

"We will see if I am any better received," Xander replied.

I held up my hand. "Could I be let in on this conversation? You know, the one accused of murder?"

"The witches of the Coven Caves are adept at using clay to create golems," Xander explained.

I tilted my head to one side. "Golems? Like big, scary clay monsters, right?"

"They are large, but not monstrous," Xander corrected me.

I shrugged. "Well, maybe Herod got some on him while he was there."

Xander shook his head. "That is possible, but not likely. The witches are very careful with their clay. They would not have tossed the clay at him so he could pass it on to you."

My face fell. "So I'm guessing we're going to go traveling."

"I will order a pair of horses for you," Mordecai offered.

"We will need three. My captain will accompany us," Xander told him.

Mordecai bowed his head. "It will be done."

I studied him with narrowed eyes. "You're pretty easy-going with this plan. Why are you even helping us?"

A thin smile spread across his lips. "Let us say I have a personal interest in your predicament."

"Yeah, you're a suspect, too," I reminded him.

Mordecai walked over and opened the door for us. He stepped to one side with the handle in his grasp and looked into my eyes. "That is true, but what choice do you have but to trust me?"

I glanced at Xander. He nodded. My shoulders slumped and I bent forward just slightly as my lips pressed together in a pout. "I guess we don't have any."

Mordecai bowed his head and swept his hand toward the doorway. "Then may I wish our new alliance good fortune."

Xander and I walked past him with me muttering some passing words. "We're probably going to need it. . ."

CHAPTER 12

Xander set his hand on the lower part of my back and directed me to the foyer of the castle. Spiros waited for us there with his hand on the hilt of his sword. Half of his attention on the soldiers who guarded either side of the front doors.

"What news?" he asked us.

Xander pursed his lips and shook his head. "Nothing good. We must travel to the Coven Caves."

Spiros arched an eyebrow. "To retrace Herod's steps?"

Xander nodded. "Among other objectives."

I raised my hand. "Could I have a bit more info on these caves? I mean, are there seriously witches there?"

A sly, crooked smile slipped onto Spiros's lips. "Having met a sorcerer, you doubt witches exist?"

TRAITORS AMONG DRAGONS

I shrugged. "I haven't really seen Mordecai do many sorcerer-y things, so yeah, I can still have a little doubt. Besides, why would Herod want to keep a bunch of witches around?"

"The witches of the Caves are proficient at curing poison," Spiros told me. "If anyone had made an attempt on Herod's life through such a design he would have surely been saved."

"So why isn't one of them here like Mordecai?" I pointed out.

"He also feared they would be the ones to poison him as they were descended from the humans who were driven ," Spiros answered as he nodded at a nearby portrait. It was of an imperious dragon lord with dark eyes like the late Herod. "Only in the time of Lord Antipater, Herod's father, was a tentative truce signed between them, but they were still never allowed near the castle."

My face fell. "Did this guy trust anyone?"

The main doors opened and a young boy of sixteen peeked into the lobby. He noticed our group and slipped over to us where he bowed his head. "Lord Xander, your horses are ready."

Xander turned to us and smiled. "Let us not keep them waiting."

The young man led us outside and to the stables that were connected to the westward wall of the castle. The building ran the entire length of the castle and held several dozen stalls. An aisle in the middle was wide enough to ride six abreast. Our three steeds stood in the aisle. Their black coats shone in the dim light of the few lanterns allowed in the hay-rich area. They threw back their heads and pawed the ground.

I skirted them and bit my lip as I watched the horses strain against their reins that were held by other stable hands. "Have these things had safety tests?"

Spiros mounted his steed and took the reins. He gave a hard tug and the horse calmed. "I would venture to say 'yes.'"

I glared at him. "Show-off. . ." A horse was brought near to me, and I reluctantly mounted the saddle. My shaking hands dropped the reins once before I got a good grip. The large animal threw its head back and eyed me with its dark gaze. I nervously smiled back. "Good horsey. Nice horsey."

The boy who summoned us drew the last horse to Xander. Behind the well-oiled saddle was a bag. Xander set his hand on the saddlebag and looked to the stable boy. "What is this?"

He shook his head. "I don't know, Your Lordship. The sorcerer asked that I pack it for you, and only said it might help for where you're going."

The connecting door to the castle opened and Blastus stepped inside. He was alone. His dark eyes fell on us and he strode over to where we were gathered. "To where are you traveling?"

Xander smiled. "To the Coven Caves. Do you wish to join us? I am sure another horse can be found." A hush fell over the quiet stable hands. They glanced at one another and pursed their lips.

Blastus stood erect and frowned. "My duties are here to attend to My Lord's body, but I might wonder why a dragon would travel to the Caves after professing innocence in Lord Herod's death."

"It is to prove that innocence that we go there," Xander told him. He mounted his horse and bowed his head. "If we have satisfied your curiosity-"

TRAITORS AMONG DRAGONS

"You have not, but I expect you will return," Blastus commented as he stepped away from our horses. His dark eyes flickered to me. "Unless your servant means less to you than you have professed."

I gripped the reins tighter and glared back at him. "We'll be back. You can count on it."

A crooked sneer slipped onto his lips. "We will see."

I wanted the last word, but Xander tugged on my reins. We turned the rears of our horses toward the jackass and trotted down the aisle. Other hands opened a pair of large doors located at the center of the stables and released us to the wilds of the blighted valley. The rain had stopped, but the dark clouds hung over us like-well, dark clouds.

Xander led the way northwestward toward the gap in the peaks. To our left and right were two other gaps. I sidled up beside Xander and nodded at them. "Where do those lead?"

He stared straight ahead and pursed his lips. "One leads to the dragon village, and the other to the remains of the human occupation."

I arched an eyebrow. "After four thousand years, how much of that is left?"

"Quite a bit," Spiros spoke up as he came up to trap me between the men. "It is said the heat of the battle was so intense the very ground was crystallized."

"It is said? You don't know?" I asked him.

"It is forbidden for anyone to travel to the eastern valley," Xander told me. He paused and furrowed his brow. "And then there are the ghosts."

I cringed. My horse threw its head back and pulled at the reins. I tugged a bit and the beast calmed before I looked to Xander once more. "Like more of the Traitor one?"

He shook his head. "No, though I have heard only stories. Amown's father told me some of the tales when I last visited the Heavy Mountains. Even if the ban was not in place, the dwarves would not venture there, even to dig under the ground for its rich resources of precious stones caused by the fire. They spoke of voices in the dark and shadows where no light was cast."

I shuddered. The beast beneath me stopped and reared up on its hind legs. I yelped and wrapped my arms around its thick neck. Its long black mane whacked me in the face and made me drop the reins. The horse, feeling the loosening of its bit, sprinted forward. Its uneven lope meant my body was jarred with every step of its hard hooves on the harder ground.

"Whoa! Whoa!" I yelled. The horse only ran faster.

Xander and Spiros came up on either side of me and leaned over with their hands outstretched as they reached for the reins. The thin ropes swung like a pendulum from one to the other, teasing them. Spiros lunged for the reins, nearly toppling over and beneath the unforgiving hooves of our beasts. His fingers twined around the thin ropes and he sat up straight. The reins pulled on the bit in my horse's mouth and the wild stallion came to a sudden halt.

Unfortunately, my stop wasn't so fast. I slid over the well-oiled saddle. Xander caught me in his arm and lowered me onto the ground. My shaking legs let me sink to the rocky surface and I pressed my palms on the ground in front of me.

Xander leapt down and knelt beside me. "Are you okay?"

TRAITORS AMONG DRAGONS

I looked up at him and managed a shaky smile. "Y-yeah. I'm just sorry I had to test out your promise to protect me."

He glanced up at my horse and frowned. "As am I." Xander stood and walked over as Spiros slipped off his own saddle. He stepped in front of the beast and took its head in his hands. The animal blinked at him. "I do not understand it. This animal should not be so skittish."

Spiros joined him by his side and held up the reins to his own steed. "Then allow me to search the animal. Your father always trusted me as the best horseman among his subjects, and my modesty has me add that it may be true of the world."

A ghost of a smile slipped onto Xander's lips. "Your modesty is admirable, but I will allow your request."

Xander took the reins of Spiros's horse and pulled the other two horses away. I followed them and together we watched Spiros work his magic. He patted down each of the horse's legs and inspected the mane, tail and saddle. The horse stood serene under the search.

Spiros moved back to the front and grasped both sides of the bit. He gave the bit a light shake. The horse's eyes shot open. It threw back its head and whinnied. Spiros grabbed the reins in both hands and pulled down. The horse was brought to its knees before him. He knelt and stroked its long nose. Its eyes half-closed and its panting subsided.

Spiros pulled out its bit and inspected the pieces of metal. He stood and turned to us with a furrowed brow. "Here is the problem." He held out the bit. Sharp bits of metal, almost too small to see, were hammered into every spot that touched the sides of the horse's mouth. "Whenever

Miriam flinched, she pulled on the reins and tugged the metal into its flesh."

Xander took the bit and turned it over in his hands. "Perhaps the sorcerer is more cunning than I anticipated."

"Or maybe that Blustering idiot came to see if I'd already broken my neck with his trick," I added.

"Did not Herod have a limp which he admitted was from a fall off a horse?" Spiros reminded us.

Xander tore off the reins and tossed the bit to the muddy ground. "Whoever is the culprit, we at least can surmise they did not want us reaching the Coven Caves."

I ran a hand through my hair as Xander threw the reins over the neck of the horse. "I wish this suspect list wasn't so long."

"We may rule out the witches. They would have no qualms with us," Spiros suggested.

Xander turned to us and shook his head. "The witches have qualms with all dragons-" he glanced at me, "-and any who side with them. If they are responsible they would not hesitate to settle the blame on Miriam."

Spiros raised the horse to its hooves and grasped the reins. "I will ride this steed, but allow me to look at the other bits and horses."

CHAPTER 13

A quick perusal found nothing amiss, and we mounted our steeds once again. The peaks came upon us in an hour and the gap opened. The barren valley of the deceased dragon lord morphed into a heavily wooded bowl. A narrow riding path meandered its way to the opposite end of the valley and the mountains that stood there. I glimpsed the faint glow of lights before we descended into the thick forest with its heavy canopy.

We rode single-file down the winding, weed-choked path. The heavy scent of brush and mold invaded my nostrils. The trees stood together in large clumps, and between those clumps was a thick growth of brush that made the ground impossible to see.

Something out of the corner of my eye caught my attention. I whipped my head to face the area. Nothing moved. A shudder ran through me, and it wasn't from the damp. "Um, guys? Do you get the feeling we're being watched?"

Spiros, who followed behind me, swept his eyes over the area. "It is more than a feeling. We are being hunted."

"Remain calm," Xander spoke up. "The forest of the witches is full of dark beasts, but they are only dangerous if they smell fear."

The color drained from my face. "Then I think we have a-" A roar sounded right beside me.

I let out a piercing scream that echoed down the trail. My horse reared up as a shadow flew from the brush and wrapped itself around the horse's neck. I was deposited into the brush, but raised my head and peeked out. My horse whinnied and bucked as it tried to dislodge the creature.

Xander unsheathed his weapon. The blue color glowed brightly in the gloomy night and illuminated the path. It also illuminated the green-colored cat-like creature that was attached to my horse.

Xander turned his horse around and sliced at the creature. The beast screamed and leapt into the darkness as something heavy dropped between my spread legs. Wet, warm blood splashed across my face. I recoiled when I saw the lump was a paw from the creature.

Spiros grabbed the reins of my terrified and bleeding steed while Xander leapt off his. The sword was at his side as he knelt beside me. "Are you safe?"

I took a deep breath. "I'm fine, but do you think they heard my scream at the Caves?"

He smiled at me. "I believe Darda heard it back in her cell."

TRAITORS AMONG DRAGONS

I frowned and smacked him on the arm. "Very funny. Now help me out of here."

Xander pulled me to my feet and over to my horse. There was a deep gash down its neck and bleeding dots where the claws had pierced its flesh. Spiros held the reins and stroked its nose.

"Will she go farther?" Xander asked him.

Spiros pursed his lips and shook his head. "Not if we wish to return with her."

A lump filled my throat. "Isn't there something we can do?"

Spiros smiled at me. "Do not fret, My Lady. A little time and a simple poultice to stop the bleeding, and I am sure she will be well enough for the return journey."

Xander looked down the trail. "The Caves are only a half hour's walk away, but someone must remain with the horses." He turned to me.

I frowned and shook my head. "Oh hell no. I'm not waiting here so that cat thing can finish the job. *You* stay here and Spiros and I will go."

Spiros laughed until Xander gave him a warning look. The captain cleared his throat. "I know you fear for her safety at the caves, Xander, but she is correct in the dangers out here."

"And I'm the only woman you've got, so I've got a better chance at not being found out," I pointed out.

Xander shook his head. "The danger is too great. The witches are not known for their hospitality toward dragons, and may finish what the beast attempted. You should remain with the horses."

I crossed my arms over my chest and sidestepped toward the creatures. They tossed their heads and snorted at me. "Do you really want me to manage the horses?"

Spiros had trouble hiding his smile. "She does have a point, Xander. These steeds are difficult to handle, and Miriam isn't knowledgeable in the making of a poultice."

I gestured to Spiros. "See? He says I'm too dumb to stay here, so I'm going with you. That is, if you have a plan to get us in there without getting killed."

Xander pursed his lips. "To be honest, I have not."

My mouth dropped open. "Seriously? No brilliant scheme or plot?"

He shook his head. "None at all."

I marched up to him and waved my hand at the forest behind me. "So you brought us here without a plan so we could become kitty chow?"

The corners of his lips twitched upward. "Not exactly. I would like for us to watch them without detection."

"Perhaps the bag from the sorcerer might prove useful," Spiros reminded us.

Xander walked over to his horse and pulled off the saddlebag off its back. He opened the leather bag and drew out a round, flat object that resembled a large facial cream container. I moved to his side as he twisted the lid off. Inside was a concoction of ashen-colored cream. Xander dipped his finger into the mixture and held it up to his face.

I took a whiff and wrinkled my nose. "What's that smell?"

Xander sniffed the stuff. "Ash of newt, if I'm not mistaken. Witches are fond of newt as an ingredient in their potions."

TRAITORS AMONG DRAGONS

He handed me the container and smeared a tiny portion of the mixture onto his wrist. Spiros's and my eyes widened as we watched his skin age several dozen years so it was as wrinkled as a basset hound. He wiped away the cream and, like a mask unveiling, the wrinkles disappeared.

Xander smiled. "It appears our new ally has given us an impressive ability to be among the witches."

"And the smell of the newt will hide your scents," Spiros added.

Xander nodded as he took more of the cream to his finger and turned to me. "If you would allow me to test the concoction further-"

I wrinkled my nose. "You know, on second thought I think I'll-" he smeared some of the cream on my cheek. I shuddered. The cream was heavy and cold.

My dragon lord proceeded with the makeup application, and soon I felt like I wore a mask. I took a look at myself in the shiny metal stirrups. I was an old crone complete with sagging eyes, crow's feet, and a pointed chin.

A snicker behind me told me the men approved of my new looks. I spun around and glared at them, especially Xander. "If you're done playing makeup, can I take this off? I'm a woman, remember? No need for a disguise."

A bemused smile graced Xander's face as he nodded. "You may."

While I wiped away the muck Xander applied the same to himself, and when he was done he closely resembled my formerly-aged appearance.

He pocketed the cream and wrapped his cloak close to himself. "Are you ready?" he asked me.

I drew my cloak around myself. "Yeah, but what if the witches realize we're strangers?"

"We will say we are visiting witches, but otherwise allow me to speak for us," he told me.

I sighed and nodded. "All right, let's do this."

CHAPTER 14

We traveled down the path and within twenty minutes had reached the end of the forest and the beginning of the foot of the mountains. Large boulders were scattered about the area and the ground was littered with rocks big and small. A meandering path made of packed stones led up the steep slope to a single doorway with a large boulder sticking out. An old woman was seated in a wicker chair beside the opening. Perched on her shoulder was a ruffled old crow.

She raised her beady eyes at us as we approached. Her voice was like nails on chalkboard. "What's wanted?"

Xander's voice sounded much the same, but squeakier. "We wish to visit our Sisters in these caves."

The woman leaned forward and eyed us. The bird squawked and readjusted itself as it, too, studied us with its black eyes. "Where are you from?"

"From the depths of Alexandria. We are of the coven of Circe," he replied.

She arched an eyebrow. "Are there many of you left?"

He nodded. "A great many. The lord is a kind and loving ruler-" I rolled my eyes, "-and allows us some protection."

"If this is true, you would know our words," she commented. She took a stick that leaned against her chair and held it out to him. "Write 'friend,' and I will allow you to enter."

The color drained from my face as Xander took the stick. He shuffled back a few steps and carefully drew the following marks in the dusty ground: friend

I stared in bewilderment at the scribblings even as the old woman stood and held out her hand to Xander. A smile lit up her wizened old face. "It is a great pleasure to see one of you again, my Sister. I have not made the acquaintance of a Circerean for many a year."

Xander bowed his head and shook her hand. "It is a pleasure to be here, Sister."

She drew back and rubbed her shaking hand. "What a powerful grasp, Sister! But let me open the way. The ceremony is about to begin, and I would not have you miss the coven of Endor at our finest." She took the stick from him and tapped one end against the boulder. The stone shuddered a moment before it rolled out of the way. We were presented with a crude tunnel lit by torches. She stepped aside and bowed to us. "May you enjoy yourselves, Sisters."

Xander smiled and returned the bow. "I am sure we will, Sister."

TRAITORS AMONG DRAGONS

He led me inside, and I jumped when the boulder shut behind us, lessening the light in the tunnel.

"Steady," he whispered in his normal voice.

I glared at his back as we shuffled along. "I'll be steady when we're gone from this place, and when you tell me how much of that back there was bullshit."

"There is a coven of witches in Alexandria, and I am familiar with their written language," he admitted.

"But you're not one of them, are you?"

"No, but I am a kind and loving ruler."

I snorted. The sound echoed off the rocky walls. "And modest. What's this stuff about Endor and Circe, anyway?"

"The witches believe their centers of worship have founders. Those of Alexandria cite a woman named Circe as their founder and those of Endor Mountain, in which we travel, cite Endora as their ancestress," he explained to me.

I wrinkled my nose. "I hope there's not going to be a test on this later. . ."

We reached an intersection that widened all four of the connected paths. The peaceful tranquility of the dark, cave-in-possible tunnel changed to an atmosphere of tense anticipation. It also got crowded. Women of all ages, from babies to the very elderly, bustled about. Many of them traveled down our path away from the entrance, and of those several cast curious glances in our direction.

Xander took my hand, and together we dove into the messy sea of cauldron-infused feminism. The passage opened into a twenty-foot wide corridor that stretched deep into the mountain. The throngs of women flowed toward an arched doorway. We reached the doorway and Xander pulled me to the side.

I glanced up at him as his eyes studied the doorway. A flickering light stretched across the floor and danced along the walls on either side of us. Through the doorway we could see a large, domed assembly room that cozily fit the five hundred witches who entered through several archways. The heavy beat of a drum kept a wickedly fast tune that thumped in time with my heart. The shadows of witches broke the torchlight as they danced around the central fire pit. A cauldron sat over the flames, and steam rose up from its boiling water. The container was just big enough to fit one dragon and one human.

I swallowed the lump in my throat and stepped backward. My back bumped against something hard. A pair of thick, stone-covered arms swung up on either side of me. I stifled a scream and stumbled forward before I spun around.

Standing before me was a six-foot tall stone creature. The form was humanoid, but there were no defining male or female features. The torso was a smooth, hulking slab with thick arms and legs attached. The head was shaped like it wore a hockey player's helmet. A pair of white, lifeless eyes stared at me.

Xander grasped my arms and leaned his lips close to my ear. "Do not be alarmed. It is merely a golem."

I snorted. "I skipped being alarmed and went straight to terrified."

"This creature is merely a stone golem. They perform strenuous labors that are too great for smaller forms," he explained.

"Are they alive?" I whispered.

"Some people believe so."

I frowned. "Then it's kind of mean to use them, isn't it?"

A woman of middle age came out from behind the creature and studied us with hard eyes. "You should know they are more reliable than any male, and twice as strong."

Xander bowed his head and pushed mine forward as he resumed his old-woman voice. "It is an honor to meet you, Priestess Endora."

The woman looked between us before her narrowed gaze settled on Xander. "I do not know your faces. Who are you?"

"Sisters from Alexandria, of the coven of-"

"Circe. I know it well." She walked up to us and glanced at me. "Do you not have any golems in your coven that you would be afraid of one?"

I swallowed and shook my head. "I-um, I'm kind of new and I just started in on the whole golem thing-"

"We have golems, but our young Sister is little used to them," Xander spoke up.

Endora tilted her head to one side and a small smile curled onto her lips as she gazed at Xander's face. "I see. And what has brought you two from the lake of Alexandria to our caves?"

Xander hunched over and leaned heavily on my shoulder. "Curiosity. I have little time left in this world, and wish to see more of my Sisters before Hecate calls me to her side."

Her eyes twinkled with mischief as she looked around us. The flow of women around us had shrank to a trickle. "Then you have come an an opportune time for we were about to begin a very great ceremony." She set her hands on the smalls of our back and turned us toward the doorway.

The golem followed behind and blocked half the passage with its girth. She twisted her head around to the few witches left and raised her voice. "Come, Sisters! Let us begin the main festivities!"

"Hoorah!" came the resounding cry from in back and in front of us.

The crowd of witches closed in on us and guided us through the doorway. The dancers spun in small circles around the cauldron as the beat of the drums grew faster. Endora led us across the room to a small, round platform. She released us and stepped onto the platform where she looked over the crowded room. The drum beat faster and faster. The women were in an ecstasy as they spun in tighter and tighter circles.

Endora raised her hands above her. The drum stopped. The dancers collapsed onto the ground. The room quieted and all eyes turned to her.

She lowered her arms and smiled at her attentive audience. "Sisters, you have all heard that the lives of the dragon man and his whore have been extinguished."

I narrowed my eyes and my jaw jutted out. "His *what?*" The whole of the audience quieted and turned to me. Xander stiffened beside me. I shrank beneath the attention and my voice was an octave higher than usual. "I mean, could you speak up? I'm a little hard of hearing."

"With the passing of the last of the dark lords we are finally able to leave the Caves as freely as our ancestors once did," she continued in a louder voice. A great cheer arose from the crowd which was only quieted by her raising her hands. "Tonight we celebrate, and tomorrow we will pick the flowers of shade on the slopes of the dragon valley!"

TRAITORS AMONG DRAGONS

There came another cheer with much clapping. Endora nodded at the drummer who resumed the pulsing beat. The old dancers stepped aside and let others take their places. More witches with handles filled with powder raced up to the fire and tossed the powder into the flames. A great burst of fire burst upward and licked the ceiling twenty feet above us. People clapped and whistled.

Endora stepped off the platform and smiled at us. "If you would remain here, Sisters, I will fetch us good things to eat."

Xander bowed. "You are too kind, Priestess Endora, but we need no special attention."

She half-turned away and coyly smiled at us over her shoulder. "Oh, but I believe you do, Sisters, and I believe someone would be very interested to speak with you. If you will wait here but a moment." She disappeared into the crowd.

Xander grabbed my hand and tugged me toward a side entrance. "We must leave."

"Like ten minutes ago. . ." I muttered as I followed him.

We stepped out of the assembly hall and into a narrow passage. Xander guided us leftward down the torch-lit hall. I looked over my shoulder. Nobody followed. "So do you know a quick way out of here?" I whispered to him.

We reached an intersection, and he looked left and right. "Unfortunately, I am not familiar with these tunnels."

I felt the color drain from my face. "So what you're saying is you don't know how to get out of here?"

"That is correct."

"I know the way."

CHAPTER 15

We both spun around to find ourselves face-to-hidden-face with a cloaked figure. The person was hunched which allowed their hood to obscure their face. Their hands were tucked into the bell sleeves in monk-like fashion.

Xander pulled me behind him. His old-woman voice was strained. "We only wished to-"

"Escape?" the figure finished for him. It was then I realized the voice was male.

A look of puzzlement slipped onto Xander's face. "Have the witches relaxed their rules on men?"

The hooded figure chuckled. "They know I am no threat to them. To you, however, I am something more."

My dragon lord leaned forward and furrowed his brow. "Euclid?"

TRAITORS AMONG DRAGONS

The figure threw off their hood and straightened to reveal himself as a young man of twenty. The man's frame was thin, but flexible. He moved with an elegance that made me mistake him for a woman. His green eyes twinkled with mischief and a smile danced across his lips. "It always was hard to fool you, Cousin."

A crooked grin slipped onto Xander's face as he strode over and grasped the man's hands in his. He gave them a good shake. "It has been a long time."

The thin man vibrated under the hard shake. He drew his hands back and rubbed them together as a smile danced across his lips. "Time hasn't dulled your strength, Cousin." He looked past Xander and nodded at me. "But who have you brought to such an adventurous place?"

Xander stepped aside and gestured to me. "This is Miriam, my Maiden."

The new dragon bowed his head to me. "It is an honor to meet you, Miriam. My cousin is fortunate in his Maiden."

I walked up to them and studied the slim figure. "So you're really Xander's cousin?"

He smiled. "Yes, a less burdened relation who's able to wander the world freely."

"Is your mother well?" Xander asked him.

Euclid nodded. "Very well, I thank you. She asked about you when I saw her two months ago. I told her you were no doubt lording very well, but I'd inquire as to your exact health if I went in that direction."

Xander arched an eyebrow as he studied his cousin. "But what has brought you here?"

I swept my eyes over the tunnel. "I hope it isn't the atmosphere."

Euclid chuckled. "On the contrary, it's the culture."

I blinked at him. "You mean the witches?"

He nodded. "Yes. I have made it my life's work to study the many cultures of humans, and as witches are one of them my wanderings brought me here. Endora was kind enough to allow me to observe them, provided she gets the last say in what I write."

I arched an eyebrow. "You had to come out here to find some humans to study?"

"Outside of the Maidens, there's very few humans left to study," he told me.

"Like how few?" I asked him.

He tilted his head back and furrowed his brow. "It's difficult to say, but perhaps no more than a half a million."

I winced. "Ouch."

Euclid pursed his lips as he nodded. "Yes. It is a great tragedy to see such an interesting race vanish from our world." He leaned toward me and studied me with a wink. "But I have heard your species thrives in your world, and you are here to assist my cousin in extending both of our lines."

I blushed and flickered my eyes to Xander. "I-um, I don't know-"

"As much pleasure as these conversations give me, might I ask how quickly the news from the castle arrived here?" Xander spoke up.

Euclid's face fell. "You're talking about the lord's death?" Xander nodded. He shrugged off the cloak and draped it over one arm. The strap of a satchel bag hung over one shoulder and its flap was tightly closed by a clasp. "I doubt it took more than a half hour after his death before the place was ringing with gossip and cackling, and only half a minute after that when the wine bottles were brought out to toast to Death." A grin slipped onto his lips as he winked at me. "You should try some before the bottles are empty."

Xander frowned. "Cousin, a lord of dragons has died, and possibly been murdered."

Euclid held up his hands in front of him. "Sorry. It's hard not to get caught up in the celebrations, especially with their wine. The Sisters make the best huckleberry wine this side of Viridi Silva."

"The castle is a ninety-minute ride from here. How did the Sisters learn of Herod's death so quickly?" Xander persisted.

"Tea leaves, or in this case the leaves of the shade plant," he replied.

"The shade plant?" I repeated.

He looked to me and nodded. "Yes. It's an old flower that grows along the northward walls of the central valley, the one with Herod's castle."

I wrinkled my nose. "I didn't see any flowers there."

"That's because it only blooms during the full moon."

"The leaves told them of his death?" Xander spoke up.

Euclid nodded. "Yep. Endora herself saw the message in her cup and informed the others." He glanced from me to Xander. "But what are you two doing here? Surely not to enjoy the celebrations."

"I'm under suspicion for killing him," I told him.

He blinked at me a moment before he snorted. "You? Are you teasing me?"

I crossed my arms over my chest and glared at him. "You don't think I could do it?"

His eyes twinkled with mischief. "There's a difference between being able and being willing. If you're truly Xander's chosen Maiden then you don't have the heart to kill anyone unless they're a danger to you." He paused and looked to Xander with a raised eyebrow. "He wasn't a danger, was he?"

Xander shook his head. "No. He called us to witness his joining with his Maiden."

Euclid pursed his lips and nodded. "Ah. That old custom. I bet she wasn't any more willing than his mom was during his. But why did you come to the Caves? If you're looking for suspects, I'm afraid the tunnels are full of them."

Xander glanced down at me. "If you would open your cloak."

I blinked at him. "Pardon?"

"To show him the mess left by Herod."

"Oh, right. That." I opened my cloak and showed off my filthy shirt. "Herod spit this out on me before he died."

Euclid leaned down and squinted. His eyes widened and flickered up to Xander. "Golem clay?"

Xander nodded. "That is what Mordecai and I believe."

Euclid straightened and snorted. "So he's still around. I'm surprised he didn't run after Herod died. The witches have always hated the sorcerers who protected Herod's line-they were always casting spells to keep them out of the central valley-but this Mordecai hasn't so much as sneezed in their direction."

"Can you tell us anything about the clay?" Xander asked him.

Euclid pinched a small clod from my shirt and turned the mess over in his palm. He furrowed his brow. "It is a very good make, the best I've ever seen."

"Then you have an idea for who might have created the clay?" Xander wondered.

Euclid half-turned away from us and jerked his head down the hall. "Follow me."

TRAITORS AMONG DRAGONS

He guided us down the hall and through the entrance into the gathering room. The witches were making their merry with dancing and wine-drinking.

"Stay here," he commanded before he strode over to the wall where Endora watched the festivities. A glass of wine was in one hand and a loaf of bread in the other. He slipped beside her and whispered into her ear.

I glanced at Xander. "So how much do you trust your cousin?"

Xander stared straight ahead at his cousin. "With my life."

"So he wouldn't kill a dragon lord to frame your Maiden, would he?" I wondered.

Xander smiled. "He is brilliant in his own way, but devilry is not in his nature. I would rather describe him as-" Euclid and Endora pushed away from the wall and walked over to us.

Xander bowed his head to the witch as she slyly smiled at him. "My apologies for the deception, Priestess Endora."

Endora laughed. "You call that a deception, dragon lord?" She nodded at his face. "The heat from the fire has half-melted your disguise."

I whipped my head up to him. His cheeks and chin were far droopier than they should have been. Xander wiped away the cream and smiled. "With such a poor disguise, you can understand I am not accustomed to deceiving others."

She waved her hand away. "Never mind. This night cannot be ruined by any deception, save for one." Her eyes flickered to Euclid and she pursed his lips. "Our dragon observer has informed me one of my witches may be involved with his death."

Xander bowed his head. "I fear such a thing is so."

She scoffed at him. "Don't mistake my intentions, dragon lord. I applaud her deed, but not that it was done without my permission nor my knowledge."

"So do you even know who made the clay?" I spoke up.

She glanced at me and gave a curt nod. "I do, and I will take you to her to confront her for I do not see her in the crowd. Come with me."

CHAPTER 16

Endora led us into the side passage and through the maze of cave tunnels. Wooden doors signaled the rooms of the witches, and many faded markings on the walls denoted their long stay there. Stairs led us down closer to the foot of the mountain. In a few minutes we stood before one of the doors. The passage was empty but for us, and at such a distance from the assembly hall all was quiet.

Endora rapped on the door. "Aphra? Are you in?" There was no reply. She tried the handle. The door didn't budge. "Aphra? Open the door!" Nothing. Endora turned to us with pursed lips. "All of you stand back."

We scattered as she stepped back and raised one of her hands. Her palm glowed a deep black like a void. A ball of black shot out and slammed into the knob. The wood burst asunder and the door swung open. We hurried inside with

Endora in the lead. The home of Aphra was a small, two-chamber area with walls that curved into the low ceiling. Simple wicker furniture sat against the walls or, as a table and chairs, in the middle of the room.

Endora strode over to the open doorway of the bedroom and looked inside. Then she turned to us. "She is not here."

Xander walked over to the table and lifted a half-finished figurine made of baked clay. It looked like the lower half of a golem. "What makes you suspect Aphra is who we seek?"

Endora joined him at the table. "She is our most gifted sculptor. It was she who made many of our golems. If that black-hearted scoundrel would seek out anyone, it would be her."

"But how would she meet him without raising suspicion?" he wondered.

She shook her head. "I do not know, but I will inquire. Shut the door when you leave." She hurried out.

Euclid stepped up to us with a small smile on his lips. "It looks like you two could use some help."

Xander set the figure down on the table and swept his gaze over the room. "I am grateful for the offer, but if the priestess cannot find her then I cannot see how you can."

"Actually, I might just know where she was meeting Herod, if she ever was," he admitted.

Xander looked to him and raised an eyebrow. "Why did you not admit as much in Endora's presence?"

Euclid scratched the back of his head and sheepishly smiled. "To be honest, I'm not supposed to know about that passage. The Sisters trust me, but not that far."

"Then please lead us-" The clay model leapt off the table and kicked me in the head.

I yelped and smacked the creature onto the ground. It climbed onto its feet, because let's face it the thing didn't have anything else, and jumped at me. Xander grabbed it and crushed the clay in his hands. The figurine crumbled into bits. He threw the remains onto the table and turned to grasp my shoulders. "Are you all right?"

I rubbed my head, but nodded. "Yeah, but that's the first time art ever judged me."

Euclid stooped and picked up a large piece. "This golem was baked to complete the spell so it would come alive."

"So we're not going to be attacked by putty creatures?" I guessed.

He stood and nodded. "That's right. The clay must be baked by magic in order to come alive."

"But why would someone bake half a creature?" I pointed out.

Xander swept his eyes over the room. "Because the creator had no time to finish her creation."

Euclid tossed the bit to the floor. "Whoever controlled the creature must be close. A golem's master can only be a hundred yards away. Otherwise, the connection is too weak even for such a small creation."

"How far is this passage?" Xander asked him.

Euclid pursed his lips. "Less than a hundred yards away."

"Then take us there."

Euclid led us from the empty chambers and through the maze of halls to the southeastern portion of the mountain. The passage ended at a dead-end. Xander looked to our guide. "Are you sure this is the passage?"

Euclid grinned as he stepped forward. "Watch this." He raised his hand to the wall. A silvery-white light emanated from his palm. The light floated forward like a swimming fish and sank into the hard rock. In a moment we heard a grinding of gears and the wall drew back to reveal a circular wooden staircase that led deeper into the ground.

Euclid lowered his arm and turned to us. "Neat, huh?"

Xander arched an eyebrow. "You have learned magic?"

Euclid folded his arms and shrugged. "Just a little. I don't really have much natural ability, but it's enough to activate the machinery on the other side of this wall."

"Is it some sort of an emergency escape?" I guessed.

He nodded. "Yes. I found out about this while I was reading one of their history books. The witches and Herod's ancestors played a long game of cat-and-mouse. When the dragons came they would spew fire into the caves, and the witches would escape through tunnels like this one." He half-turned and studied the wall. "It took me forever to find one of the passages, but it didn't take me long to open it."

"Why is that?" I asked him.

He returned his attention to us and pursed his lips. "Though Herod's family haven't attacked in a century, the machine was recently greased. I found the oil can beside the mechanism. The stairs were also fixed."

Xander took a torch off a nearby wall and strode past us. "Let us see if we can discover those who use this passage."

Euclid and I followed Xander down the winding stairs. We paused to shut the wall behind us, and with me in the middle we continued on our way. The steps took us fifty feet deeper into the ground and to a new, roughly-cut passage. Jagged points of stone stuck out of the walls and the ceiling rose and fell. Xander raised above his head and cast the light several dozen feet in front of us, but we still couldn't see the end.

"There aren't any chambers or side-passages. This tunnel was one of the ancient escape points for the humans who survived the assault on their castle. It just leads to the end," Euclid told us.

"And where's that?" I asked him.

He looked past me at Xander. "The Forbidden Valley."

Xander pursed his lips and glanced back down the passage. "We have no choice. The murderer must be caught, and your name cleared. We will go forward."

My dragon lord hurried along, and Euclid and I followed. I glanced over my shoulder at my new acquaintance. "So if you went to the Forbidden Valley that means it isn't as bad as people make it out to be, right?"

A dark shadow passed over his face and he lost a little color. "What have you been told?"

I shrugged. "Just that there might be ghosts."

He looked past me at the way ahead. "There are the ghosts, and then there are the other things."

I raised an eyebrow. "'Things?'"

He shook off his pensive mood and shook his head.. "I'm not sure. My expertise lies with the cultural world, not the spiritual or magical realms."

"But you know how to do magic," I reminded him.

He nodded. "I know a little, but I wouldn't want to rely on it to save my life, or anyone else's."

My shoulders drooped and I looked ahead. "Perfect..."

Xander stopped so quickly I crashed into his back and Euclid into mine. My dragon lord pushed his toes against the ground and kept us from falling forward.

Euclid straightened and leaned to one side to see Xander. "What's the matter?" Xander raised his torch and revealed a dark, arch-shaped shadow twenty feet ahead of us. Euclid frowned. "A passage?"

Xander half-turned and looked to his cousin. "You told us there were no side-passages."

Euclid shook his head. "There wasn't. This must have been dug recently."

"When were you last down here?"

"Only two weeks ago."

Xander pursed his lips and moved forward, but at a slow pace. We reached the arch and found it was a perfectly-shaped entrance into a perfectly carved tunnel. The passage only reached ten feet before it met its end in a small room. Xander's torchlight reflected off the life-size faces of a half-dozen golems. I yelped and jumped behind him.

Euclid chuckled. "It's all right, they aren't awake."

I peeked out from behind my dragon and studied the things. Their eyes didn't have the white glow like the one from near the assembly hall. "That must take a lot of clay to make those sizes."

He shook his head. "No more than the one that attacked you. A golem is a solid mass of clay when it is fired by magic. Once it becomes a moving creature the master may stretch the block of clay to nearly skin-thin. Thus the creature becomes the size of a human, or they might shrink it back to something they might carry with them."

"Huh. So a portable servant," I commented as I nodded at the creatures. "So did they dig this tunnel?"

TRAITORS AMONG DRAGONS

Euclid swept his eyes over the smooth walls. "There's no question a dwarf dug this."

Xander pressed his hand "But for what purpose is the question."

"Maybe it was Herod. After all, the dwarves work for him and if he attacked anybody he would've done it in a sneak attack," I pointed out.

Xander stooped and brushed his hand over the footprints. His eyes followed the footprints down the tunnel and he shook his head. "These footprints do not match the soles of the boots worn by Herod's men."

I crossed my arms and arched an eyebrow. "You studied their bootprints?"

Xander stood and shook his head. "No, but the pattern of this footwear does not correspond to any boots I have ever seen."

I squinted at the prints. The flickering light from the torch didn't help me much. "They just look like normal footprints to me."

My lord partially turned to me and raised an eyebrow. "They are not foreign to you?"

I shook my head. "No, why do you-" My eyes widened as the realization hit me. I snatched the torch from Euclid and knelt down in front of one of the prints. A quick, intense look told me the rubber soles were very familiar to me. "Okay, these definitely belong to a pair of sneakers."

"'Sneakers?'" Euclid repeated.

I raised my head to look at him and nodded. "Yep. They're pretty much the lingua franca of the shoe world in my old world, if you'll pardon my French." I received a pair of blank stares from my dragon companions. My eyes rolled as I sighed. "These shoes are worn by a bunch of people in my world. Got it?"

"Then perhaps Herod's Maiden found the tunnel and explored its depths before their demise?" Euclid suggested.

Xander shook his head. "He would have insisted on the destruction of her human-world clothes, including her footwear."

I shrugged. "Maybe the footwear wasn't destroyed. Maybe somebody decided they liked them and kept them for themselves."

Xander pursed his lips as he studied the prints. "Unfortunately, with the Maiden dead that will be difficult to prove."

"And even more difficult to prove these prints have anything to do with Herod's death," Euclid added.

I furrowed my brow as a memory came to me. "But why would anybody want to steal Olivia's old shoes and use them here?"

Xander stood and turned to me. "Why do you believe they were stolen?"

"Olivia told me she wasn't allowed to leave the castle. Herod wouldn't let her even go outside to climb the trees," I explained.

Xander raised an eyebrow. "Are these 'sneakers' very specific to the wearer's feet?"

I shrugged. "That depends on the foot size."

He swept his eyes over the golems. "And these feet are very small."

That's when the golems woke up.

CHAPTER 17

The dark niches in their heads where their eyes should have been lit up like white Christmas lights. They stretched out their fat hands and reached for us. Xander drew me behind him and sliced the air in front of him. His hands were now taloned claws and the dagger-like fingers cut into the hands. His effort only produced deep gashes. The creatures lost nothing, even the momentum as they marched faster toward us. He threw his torch at them and spun around to face us.

"Run!" Xander ordered.

I turned, but was summarily thrown over Xander's shoulder. I got a great view of the golems behind us. Their hefty bodies belied a speed that would have outran me as they kept pace with the dragons. One of them stopped and smashed both fat fists against the leftward wall. The passage shook and I heard a crash in front of us.

I looked over my shoulder and saw rocks fall down, blocking our way back to the Coven Caves. Euclid was in the lead and took a sharp right further down the passage. Xander followed, and close at our heels were the monsters. Their white eyes shone brightly in the long, dark corridor as boots and clay feet pounded the hard rock. With every twenty feet the golems lost one so they started to fall behind.

They didn't like that. Two stopped and smashed their fists against both walls. Dirt and rocks rained down on us. I ducked my head to keep the choking dust from my face. Xander and Euclid slipped on the loose stones that littered the floor, but our foes weren't deterred. The golems kept their pounding as the other four gained on us.

"How much farther?" Xander choked out amid all the falling dust and dirt.

"Not much farther!" Euclid shouted.

I raised my head and my eyes widened. One of the golems was only five feet off. Its fat, grubby hands reached for me. "Too far!"

The passage crumbled as the two golems caved in the walls around us and them.

"I need some time to open the hatch!" Euclid told us.

"One moment!" Xander replied.

Xander spun around and stretched out his arm at the same time. His fist removed the golem's head from its body. The creature stumbled and fell chest-first onto the ground. Its massive form blocked the others and forced them to climb over its body, slowing down their pursuit.

We sped down the passage and caught up to Euclid. He stood at a closed wall and his arm outstretched above him. The end of the passage shifted and slid to the left into the wall. The outside world was revealed, and it was bleak. Dark clouds hung over the jagged-peaked scenery, and far below us was a black valley of ruined stone foundations.

Far, far below us. The doorway was located a hundred feet above the valley floor on a steep slope. At the bottom were piles of scattered boulders and rocks. A small ledge was all that separated the living from the dead.

Euclid stepped up to the edge and half-turned to us. His wings burst from his back and tore through this shirt to flap behind him. "We have to jump!"

"Are you crazy?" I asked him.

"Hold your position!" Xander ordered him.

I whipped my head over my shoulder to stare at my dragon lord. "Are *you* crazy?"

Moans from behind us reminded me of the pros of jumping. The three remaining golems rushed us. Xander stepped up beside Euclid and spread open his leathery wings. "Jump on my call!" The creatures were only ten feet away. He shifted me to his arms. Five. "Jump!"

Euclid and Xander leapt into the abyss. My scream echoed down the valley walls as we fell down the same. The dragon men opened their wings to their full width as our clay foes tumbled over the precipice and down the steep slope. A breeze slowed our descent and lifted us above them. We had a great view as they crashed into the boulders and broke into chunky pieces.

The dragons landed some fifty feet from the boulder field. Xander set me down and we all turned to look at the rocks. Moans and spasms arose from the mounds of our fallen foes. Random hands, half detached from their bodies, waved back and forth. A tinge of pity stabbed at my heart.

Xander set his hands on my shoulders. His fingers were long, thick talons. "Remain here. I will put them to rest." He dropped his hand and strode over to the twitching masses of clay.

I turned my face away as he destroyed the crumbled remains of the creatures. My eyes fell on the blackened foundations. In the center of the ruins was a hulking mound of blackened dirt.

A chill sank into my bones. I wrapped my arms around myself and looked around. Nothing stirred. "It's so quiet. . ." I whispered. Anything louder would have been a sacrilege.

Euclid tilted his head back to look at the dark sky. His lips were pressed tightly together as his eyes scanned the heavy clouds "Though the birds can fly on Heavy Mountains they won't venture into this valley."

I glanced at a nearby foundation. "So this is where the humans made their stand against the dragons?" Euclid didn't reply. I looked to him and found his expression tense. I winced. "Sorry. I didn't mean for it to come out like that."

He shook his head. "No, you're quite right to put it in those terms. Dragons have a long history, and not all of it is something we can be proud of. As for your question, yes, this is the valley in which the humans." He nodded at a tall wall at the farther end of the valley beyond the mound. "That's where the castle once stood."

"And the mound?" I wondered.

"That is the burial mound for the dragons who fell."

I glanced at him. "And the humans who died?"

He closed his eyes and shook his head. "Their bodies were left to the elements."

TRAITORS AMONG DRAGONS

The soft breeze that guided us down to the valley floor now blew over me as a chill wind. A distant sound like a deep groan came to my ears. "Cheery thought."

We stood among that heavy silence until the last golem stopped moving. Xander stepped out of the boulder field and over to us. He hid his wings, but not his claws, before he looked to his cousin. "What do you make of those golems?"

Euclid pursed his lips. "Their designs were standard, but their strength and speed show that they were made by a mistress of the craft."

"This missing witch was such a mistress?" Xander asked him.

Euclid nodded. "Yes, and my few interactions with her told me she had less liking for dragons and men than the average witch."

Xander swept his gaze over the ruins. "Then we may assume she is not far-" I screamed as a slender, orange-colored hand broke through the surface and grabbed my ankle. The fingers were long and ended in sharp points.

Xander leapt down and sliced the hand off at the wrist. He drew me away as more hands burst from the ground and drew their bodies up after them. The creatures were golems, but their figures were more slender than mine and their features were curvier like that of a woman. They totaled two dozen slim, clay fighting machines.

Xander, Euclid and I pressed our backs together as the golems surrounded us. "Great. I'm going to be killed by a bunch of models. . ." I muttered.

Euclid dipped his hands into his satchel and drew out a slingshot and a bunch of glowing balls the size of marbles. "Not quite, Miriam."

Xander glanced over his shoulder at Euclid and his balls. "Catastrophe Orbs?"

Euclid grinned and nodded. "Yep. I made them myself."

"What does that mean?" I asked them.

Xander returned his attention to the golems and smiled. "It means we may have a chance at-" Our foes drew their lips back and revealed long sharp teeth through which they hissed.

Half the golems leapt at us. Their movements were as lithe as ballerinas and as fast as Olympic-class sprinters. They stretched out their hands and pressed their fingers together to stab us. Xander drew his sword and sliced off the hands. They flopped to the ground, but that didn't stop the momentum of the creatures. They swung their arms at him, and he blocked and punched their heads from their shoulders.

Euclid raised his slingshot and fired the balls so quickly I could barely see his movements. The balls hit the creatures in their faces and exploded in a brilliant flash of rainbow-colored light. The headless bodies staggered a few steps before they collapsed to the ground.

I wasn't so gallant, or really that helpful. I ducked and dodged the creatures until the men took care of it. One of them caused me to trip over my own feet and fall flat on my back. The soul stone in my pocket jabbed into my hip. I pulled it out and thrust it into the face of one of the hissing creatures. The creature started back and blinked at the green-glowing ball.

I shook the ball. "Come on! Do something amazing! Or just helpful!"

The golem lady snarled and lunged at me. Xander came up and lopped off its head. The detached noggin dropped between my legs and its white eyes dimmed to nothing. I cringed and kicked it away.

My dragon lord turned to me with a smile and held out his hand. "I will keep my word to protect you."

I grinned and clapped my hand into his. "I wouldn't have it-" Something moved past him. A flicker of a shadow behind one of the few remaining walls.

Xander released my hand and spun around just as a tiny, slim object flew out from behind the wall. It was a small dart aimed at me. Xander leapt into its path and took the dart full in the chest.

Xander staggered back and fell to his knees. Bucephalus clattered to the ground.

CHAPTER 18

"Xander!" I cried out before I lunged for him as he teetered back.

I caught him in my arms as Euclid turned to me. His gaze followed where Xander and I faced. He aimed his slingshot and fired in the direction from where the dart had come. The ball hit the base of the wall behind which I'd seen the figure. The explosion caused the stones to teeter and topple over. I heard a scream before it was cut short by the crashing stones.

The remaining golems stopped. Their glowing eyes disappeared and they collapsed to the ground as nothing more than piles of clay.

Xander groaned in my arms. I looked down and saw his eyes roll back. His body started to tremble. I whipped my head up. "Euclid!"

TRAITORS AMONG DRAGONS

Euclid hurried over and slid down beside me. He ripped open Xander's shirt and revealed the depth of the needle. A good three inches lay in Xander's chest.

Euclid dropped his bag on the ground beside us and rummaged through it. "Hold him as still as you can. I think I know what poison this is."

"Do you want me to pull the needle out?" I offered.

He shook his head. "No. Pulling out the needle without the antidote will kill him. Just keep him still."

My heart quickened with each shallow, strained breath from Xander. Euclid drew out a vial and popped the cork. He scooted close and grabbed Xander's chin. "He's going to fight this pretty hard, so get ready." I nodded.

Euclid pulled Xander's jaw down and stuffed the mouth of the vial into the mouth of the victim. Half the contents had spilled down Xander's throat before his body started to thrash. I pressed him against my chest and clenched my teeth as I struggled to keep him still. The dragon's strength meant I didn't have much to show for my effort.

Euclid finished the medicine and tossed aside the vial before he pressed Xander to the ground. Xander convulsed for a few moments longer before the tremors sank into shivers and then stopped altogether. Xander's head fell back against my chest and the rest of his body slid to the ground.

"Hold him in your arms while I get the needle out in case more poison gets into him," Euclid told me.

I cradled Xander in my arms as Euclid grasped the needle in one hand. He pressed the palm of the other hand against Xander's chest, and with a quick jerk he pulled the needle free. Xander's chest jumped up and he hissed through his teeth before he dropped back into my arms. His breathing was a little quick, but otherwise normal. Euclid set the needle in his bag and shut the satchel.

I lifted my eyes and met Euclid's strained gaze. "Will he. . .will he be all right?" I choked out.

Euclid leaned back and nodded. "Yes, but five more minutes and even I couldn't have saved him."

I snorted and adjusted Xander's great weight. "It's a good thing you were here. I think I'm too tired to cry."

Euclid smiled. "No need for tears just yet, but we should wait to celebrate, as well." He glanced over at the destroyed wall. "Stay here. I'm going to go see what that noise was." He stood and, with his slingshot at his side, walked over to the wall.

I looked around at the golems and from where they had originated. They'd been hidden in deep, perfectly shaped rectangular pits that were just deep enough to cover their bodies if they were crouched down. They had broken through a mesh of wicker covered in plates of mud made from the ground around us.

Noise brought my attention back to Euclid. Stones clattered to the ground as he dug through the remains of the wall. He tossed a large one aside and paused. A shadow passed over his face as he knelt down and reached into the hole hidden by the stone. He closed his eyes and shook his head before he stood and returned to me.

I looked up into his dire face. "What was it?"

He knelt beside me and looked at Xander's ashen face. "The witch, Aphra."

I swallowed the lump in my throat. "Is she-?"

He didn't look at me when he nodded. "Yes, she's dead."

TRAITORS AMONG DRAGONS

I pressed my lips together and set my hand atop his. "You did it to save us."

Euclid raised his head and managed a small smile. "Thank you for that small comfort, Miriam." Xander shifted in my arms and his eyes fluttered open. "And speaking of whom I have saved."

Xander blinked up at us. His eyes settled on me and he grasped my hand. "Are you. . .are you safe?"

I smiled and nodded. "Yep, thanks to you and Euclid."

He set his eyes on his cousin. "Thank you for saving her."

He shrugged. "Don't mention it. Really. Besides, I solved one problem and made another. Aphra's dead so we can't ask her why she did what she did."

Xander sat up and winced. "I may have an idea who is behind these troubles."

"Shouldn't you be holding still for a little while?" I scolded him.

He chuckled as he slowly climbed to his feet. "You forget I am a dragon lord, and dragon lords are-" His legs shook under him and if I hadn't tucked myself under one of his arms his face would have made the acquaintance with the ground.

"-are very stubborn," I finished for him.

Euclid stood and swept his eyes over the hidden holes. "Whoever is behind this paid a high price. The dwarves would not have otherwise dug so many pits without a fair amount of gold and gems in it for them."

"Or perhaps a piece of jewelry," Xander suggested. He straightened and his legs didn't wobble. "But we must return to the castle."

The color drained from my face. "Can you prove I didn't do it?"

He nodded. "I believe I can, at least to the satisfaction of Mordecai, and he will convince the captain."

I looked around us at the devastation. The opening to the central valley was a couple of miles away, and beyond that was another couple dozen miles to the castle. The geography between here and there was a flat wasteland of blackened rock.

I glanced back to my dragon lord. "So how do we get back there?"

Xander knelt down. "We will use our wings, and you will be on my back."

I blinked at him. "But you can't fly up here."

He smiled. "But we may still glide."

Euclid stepped up to us. "I think I should take her. You were just poisoned by a witch."

Xander shook his head. "I appreciate the gesture, but Miriam's presence will give me the strength to glide there."

"But how are we going to glide when the trail is flat?" I pointed out.

He tilted his head up and caught my eyes. "Trust me."

My shoulders sagged and I sighed. "All right, but I better not end up screaming."

I climbed onto Xander's back and he stood. He glanced over his shoulder at me. "Comfortable?"

I shifted and winced. "I wish you came with seat belts." He blinked at me. I patted him on the shoulder. "Let's just get going."

Xander led Euclid across the blackened valley to the gap between the central and Forbidden valleys. They slammed their taloned hands into the thick rock and climbed

128

up the steep slope. The ground grew farther and farther, and we soon were able to see the entirety of both valleys. We reached three-quarters of the way up the mountain before the dragons unfurled their wings.

Xander glanced at Euclid. "Do you have faith you can glide to the castle?"

Euclid nodded. "I think I can do it, but are you sure you can carry Miriam?"

Xander turned around so I was between his back and the mountain. "I have no choice."

He opened his wings and flexed them. A soft breeze rippled against the leather. He tensed his body to push off from the mountain. I glanced to our left for one final view of the Forbidden Valley. Shadows lurked around every wall and stone. Some of them shifted. Maybe it was the weak light, but their forms took on a strangely human shape.

Xander pushed off and we flew away from those dark shades. Euclid glided by our side, and the vast central valley swept under us. The wind carried us over the gnarled branches of the trees and close to the castle walls. The movement of the guards on the battlements told us we'd been spotted.

Xander and Euclid landed on their feet and I dropped down. The castle stood a hundred yards off. A contingent of guards stepped out and marched over for a warm, sword-wielding greeting.

At the head of the group was the captain himself, Blastus. He stopped ten feet short of our group and glared at us. His hand lay on the hilt of his sword and his eyes settled on Euclid. "Who is this?"

Euclid smiled and bowed to him. "Euclid, of the House of Alexandros. If you'll recall, I passed through here some months ago."

Blastus turned his attention to Xander. "Have you returned merely to make reintroductions?"

My dragon lord shook his head. "No, to clear my Maiden's name and to free my servant."

Blastus arched an eyebrow. "Then you have proof?"

Xander's eyes flickered over the other guards. "It is a matter I prefer to speak of in private."

Blastus pursed his lips, but half-turned away from us and jerked his head toward the castle. "Come with us."

We were back, and we were still in trouble.

CHAPTER 19

We were marched back to the castle. The guards stuck close to us. I nervously eyed Xander. His expression was tense.

Mordecai met us in the courtyard. "What news?" he asked us.

"I ask for a private meeting with Blastus and yourself," Xander pleaded.

The sorcerer glanced at the captain. "Would my chambers suffice?"

Blastus nodded. Mordecai led us to the chamber from before with the books and mess. He opened the door and stepped inside with Blastus close behind.

Euclid and I stepped forward to follow, but Xander held out his arm and blocked our path. "Remain out here. This will not be long."

I frowned. "But-"

"Trust me."

I crossed my arms over my chest and pressed my lips together. "Fine, but hurry it up, will you? If the anticipation doesn't kill me, Blastus might."

Xander bowed his and followed the others into the chamber. The door shut. Euclid and I were left with the stiff, silent guards.

I glanced at Euclid. "Has Xander always been this cocky?"

He smiled as he watched the door. "Haven't you found him to be reliable?"

"Yeah, but-"

"And a man of his word?"

"Yeah, I guess-"

"His confidence stems from the faith in himself, and the faith others have in him," Euclid told me. His teasing eyes flickered down to me. "And his love for a certain woman drives him to be an even better man."

A faint blush warmed my cheeks and I turned my face away. "I guess I'll take that excuse. . ."

The minutes ticked by. I tapped my foot on the ground as my heart thumped hard in my chest. Nobody moved. Everyone watched the door.

After thirty minutes the door opened. Everyone tensed. Xander stepped out and walked over to us. He grasped my hands and looked into my eyes. "It is done."

I searched his face to decrypt his words. "What's that supposed to mean?"

He smiled and nodded. "Everything is as I hoped."

We all looked to the doorway as Mordecai and Blastus exited the room. Mordecai's eyes flickered to Blastus. The stoic captain walked up to us, and his eyes fell on me. "Miriam, Maiden of Xander the Sixth Alexandros, you are hereby charged with the murder of Our Lord Herod."

Xander's eyes widened and his voice roared over the room. "What?"

Guards swarmed us as Blastus stepped back. "Do not make this difficult for everyone. Any attempts to flee will be met with death for you all."

Several of them grabbed me and tore me from Xander's grasp. He lunged for my hand, but they grabbed him and yanked him away. He whipped his head around to glare at Blastus and Mordecai. "You lied to me!"

"We are unconvinced by your story," Mordecai corrected him.

"Release her! She is innocent!" Xander demanded.

"We will release her for her execution if you can prove she is otherwise not guilty," Blastus told him.

Xander strained against his captors. "But I told you what had happened, and who is responsible!"

Euclid marched forward, but was blocked by other guards. "You have to believe us! Whatever Xander told you is the truth!"

"We will look into this matter further, but in the meantime the Maiden must be kept in the dungeon," Mordecai insisted.

The guards dragged me away from my friends and down the hall to the dungeon stairs. I stumbled and tripped down the steps, but they pushed me along between them. We hurried down the cell passage to my previous abode.

Darda stood at the bars of her cell. Her eyes widened as I was shoved past. She stretched out her hands to grab me, but the guards slapped them down.

One of the guards stopped at her cell and opened the door. Darda tried to slip around him and follow me, but he grabbed her arm and shoved her toward the stairs. "Not that way. You're to be upstairs."

"But what's going on? What's happened?" she asked him.

He shoved her further away as I was pushed into my cell. "Move."

"Miriam!" she shouted.

One of the guards slammed the door behind me. I turned and grasped the bars. "I'm okay! Just get Xander to think of a better plan!"

"I will! I swear it!" she called out before the guard pushed her upstairs.

The others followed them. The chinking noise of their metal disappeared, and I was left in a stony silence. I shuffled over to the hard bed and plopped myself on its cold top. "Stupid dragons. . ." I muttered as I cupped my chin in one hand. "First in the dungeon, then out of the dungeon, now back in the dungeon."

"They are, aren't they?"

I leapt to my feet and spun around to face the bars of my cell. There, standing at the cell door, was Olivia. She was attired in her normal, human-world clothes. A sly grin was on her face as she grasped the bars. "You have no idea how funny you look right now."

I pointed a shaking finger at her. "B-but you're dead."

She shook her head. "Nope, but wasn't it great? I couldn't believe how life-like that golem thing was, especially after we put that black dress on it."

I furrowed my brow. "That-Herod was Joined to a golem?"

TRAITORS AMONG DRAGONS

Olivia leaned against the bars and grinned. "Neat, huh? He puts his heart in a piece of clay and then WHAM! Judith smashes it."

My eyes widened. "Judith? But why would his servant want to kill him?"

She turned her face away and frowned. "More like a slave. He got what he deserved with all the abuse he gave both of us." She scoffed and glanced back to me. "Only the dwarves had to be paid off to dig all these tunnels, but all they wanted was that stupid necklace Herod gave me."

I glared at her and shook my head. "You think you're all great for killing someone, but you're not."

She sneered at me. "That's easy for you to spout. You were given to a great dragon. I got shafted-"

"You got who you deserved," I snapped.

Olivia's lips curled back in a snarl and her voice rose to a higher volume. "I deserved just as much as you got!" Her voice echoed down the passage. She clapped her hand over her mouth and her eyes flickered down the hall in the direction of the stairs. Nothing stirred. She lowered her hand and grinned as she returned her attention to me. "You know, I never thought I'd like being without electricity, but for once it's pretty useful. Nobody to overhear us talking, and nobody to hear you scream."

I stepped back as she drew out a small pipe and a dart from her coat. "I got this from that witch, Aphra. She's pretty handy with these things."

My back hit the wall as my mind tried to bide time. "Did you know she was also dead?" I asked her.

Olivia paused and looked up at me. "Really?"

I nodded. "Really. We killed her in the Forbidden Valley."

Olivia shrugged and loaded the dart into the blow gun. "That's all right. The Crimson guy got what he wanted out of her. He just asked me to take care of you and then he'd get me out of here."

My eyes flickered to the right-hand side of the cell. The lower part of my dress lay on the floor. I inched toward it as she studied the blow gun. "What Crimson guy?"

"I don't know. He's some guy Judith met." She raised the dart gun so it pointed at my chest and pressed her lips against the other end. Her voice had a hollow ring to it as it traveled down the pipe. "There's not really anything else to tell you except good-" A flurry of heavy feet raced down the stairs.

Olivia lowered the pipe and whipped her head in the direction of the steps. I leapt forward and grabbed the dress as she turned back to me. I threw one end of the cloth through the bars and around her neck. She dropped the pipe and tried to pull back as I grabbed the loose end. I drew the cloth farther down to her waist and yanked toward me. Olivia slammed against the bars and stuck there.

"Let me go, you asshole! Let me go!"

Xander with all my friends and acquaintances rushed into the hall. A group of guards followed behind them. Olivia was surrounded and grabbed. I let the cloth drop to the ground and stepped back.

Xander himself unlocked the cell with keys from a guard and hurried inside. He wrapped me in a tight hug as he glared at Olivia. Two of the guards held her arms behind her as Blastus moved to stand in front of her.

His dark eyes glared down at the captive Maiden. "So it was you all this time. My Lord's dying words rang true, but not for the Maiden we thought."

TRAITORS AMONG DRAGONS

She sneered at him. "What do you care?" She swept her eyes over the company. "What do any of you care? He was a disgusting, horrible dragon! You all hated him! Don't deny it! I did you all a favor!"

Blastus narrowed his eyes. "He was cruel as all his line before him, but he was our lord, and for his murder our laws demand we give you a fit punishment."

The color drained from Olivia's face. "And what's that?"

"The punishment is death by beheading."

Olivia's eyes widened. She shook her head. "No. No, you can't. I-I was just being used! I have info I can give to you!"

Blastus shook his head. "You yourself admitted all to this other Maiden." He looked past her at the guards. They grabbed her arms and pulled her away.

Olivia thrashed and pulled backward. Her eyes fell on me and stretched out her hand in my direction. "Miriam! Miriam, you have to help me!" I pursed my lips and turned my face away. Her screams dug into me. "Miriam! Don't let them do this! Miriam!"

I winced and bit my lower lip. Xander looked to Blastus. "What of her confederate?"

I looked up at him and frowned. "Judith? But how'd you know?"

"She will be found and receive the same punishment," Blastus promised. He turned his attention to me and bowed his head. "For all I have done and all I have said, I apologize."

I shook my head. "I'd just like to know how *you guys* know about Judith."

Xander nodded at Mordecai who stood near the wall opposite the cell. "Though we have no electricity, in this instance magic suited the same purpose. Mordecai allowed us to watch and listen through his Gazer."

I blinked at him. "'Gazer?'"

"A crystal ball," Darda explained.

A tiny, squeaking mouse appeared from the left of my cell. Mordecai leaned down and allowed the mouse into his palm. He straightened and held the creature in his hand in front of him. I grinned. "I thought you said there weren't any mice down here."

He smiled. "Only those that I allow, and only when I need them to be my eyes and ears."

I pointed at the rodent. "That's what you used to watch us?"

He pocketed the creature and bowed his head. "Yes."

I stepped outside the cell and shook my head. "I don't think I'll ever get used to this-" My eyes caught on something at the end of the passage. It was a small hatch-like doorway in the wall. I glanced over my shoulder at Xander who followed behind me. "Is that how Olivia got in here?"

Xander nodded. "Yes. For the price of such a precious necklace, the dwarves risked Herod's wrath and dug that tunnel and the others."

I winced. "Is anything going to happen to them?"

"For now, their treasure will be confiscated and they will be barred from entering the castle," Blastus replied.

Xander set his hands on my shoulders. "And in the meanwhile, we will find some rest in our rooms."

I sighed. "Amen to that."

CHAPTER 20

Our group left Blastus to carry on his retribution against those who harmed Herod. We stopped in front of my chamber door and I looked to Mordecai. "I've been meaning to ask you something."

He bowed his head. "Ask me what you wish."

"How come you were so sure I didn't kill Herod? I mean, all the evidence pointed at me," I pointed out.

Mordecai raised his head and a small, crooked slipped onto his lips. "Let us say your experience is not unique to our world." He grabbed the red band around his neck and gave a tug. The cloth band fell from his neck and revealed a band of scarred flesh.

Xander stiffened at my side. "You are a condemned?"

Mordecai nodded. "Yes. I, too, was framed for a murder I did not commit. My punishment was death by hanging, and it was carried out with cruel efficiency. Only my powers kept my neck from breaking. That is where Herod's men found me, alive and swinging from the gallows. He offered me a sanctuary, but at a price. I was to obey him and he would not betray me to my foes."

I cringed. "Then that mark was left by a hangman's noose?"

"It was, but now that I am free of Herod's iron grasp I see that I must now set the world right and find justice for myself." Mordecai bowed his head to us. "I hope we will meet again."

Xander returned the gesture. "May you find your justice."

Mordecai turned and walked away. I glanced at Xander. "You think he's telling the truth about not being a murderer."

Xander smiled and turned us toward the door. "You of all people should appreciate some doubt to a person's guilt."

I winced. "Touche."

Darda grasped the handle of the door behind us and smiled. Euclid waved at us from behind her. "We will leave you two alone to rest. Goodnight."

The moment she shut the door Xander slid his arms around me. I stepped out of his grasp, spun around, and placed my hands on my hips. "You really think I'm going to let you do that?"

He blinked at me. "Have I done something wrong?"

I snorted. "I'd say. Why didn't you warn me about the trap?"

He stepped closer to me and set his hands on my hips. "I needed a convincing reaction from you. Otherwise, the trap would have failed."

TRAITORS AMONG DRAGONS

I leaned back and narrowed my eyes. "How did you even know the trap would work?"

"The attempt on your life on the horse and in the Forbidden Valley showed me that whoever was our foe, their main objective was to kill you," he explained.

My mouth dropped open. "So you used me as live bait hoping they'd try it again?"

He nodded. "Yes."

I glared at him and tried to shrug off his arms. "Some dragon lord you are! Just toss your Maiden to the wolves, why don't ya!"

Xander chuckled and leaned down to nuzzle me behind my ear. "I promised I would protect you."

My shoulders fell, but I stuck out my jaw. "Well, next time don't cut it so close, okay? She was taking in breath to shoot that thing, you know."

"I assure you no horse could have ran swifter than I in getting to you," he told me.

"That's not the-" I froze. "Uh-oh."

He drew away from me and looked into my face. "What is it?"

I looked up at him. "I think we forgot about something."

Xander raised an eyebrow. "Another foe?"

I shook my head. "No, worse. An ally. Spiros. We left him in that forest, remember?"

Xander's eyes widened. He spun around and marched to the door where we found Euclid on the other side leaning against the wall opposite the door. He jumped to attention. "What's the matter? In need of a nightcap?"

Xander shook his head. "No, two horses. I left Spiros in the woods before Coven Caves."

Euclid grinned. "He won't let you live that down."

"We shall see if we find him in such a state," Xander replied as he strode past him.

In a little over an hour Xander, Euclid, Darda and I arrived at the spot where we left Spiros. The bright flames from a fire signaled our friend was well, but he wasn't alone. The horses stood off to one side, and on the opposite side of the camp were a half dozen bodies of the forest cats stacked neatly beside the path.

Spiros stood as we galloped up to him and swept his eyes over our large group. His gaze settled on Darda and Euclid before he looked to Xander. "Am I correct to assume the troubles are past?"

Xander dismounted and nodded. "You are correct."

"And that I was forgotten in the excitement?"

"Again, you are correct."

"And that I shall be knighted *again* for my patience?"

"If you wish it."

"What about a small portion of your kingdom, My Lord?"

"That is taking things too far, captain."

Spiros grinned. "You cannot blame a lowly captain for trying, but how did the adventure end? In a battle for-" A slight rustling in the woods alerted us to danger.

Xander pushed me behind him and unsheathed his weapon while the others did the same. I was surrounded by a small, protective arsenal of two swords, a slingshot, and a dagger. The brush in front of us parted and a woman stepped out. She was followed by two dozen more, all led by Endora.

TRAITORS AMONG DRAGONS

Her hard eyes fell on Euclid and Xander. "We, too, wish to know the whole story before you leave the mountains."

Euclid stepped forward and held out his empty hands. "We had no intention to leave without conference with you, Priestess Endora. We came to fetch our friend and tell you that you can find Aphra's body in the Forbidden Valley."

A dark murmuring arose from the witches. Endora raised her hand and silenced them before she returned her attention to Euclid. "What was she doing there?"

"Trying to kill us," I piped up.

Endora arched an eyebrow. "Do you have proof of this?"

"One moment and I'll show you," Euclid spoke up. He rummaged through his bag and drew out the dart which he handed to Endora. "She shot Xander with this, and meant the dart for his Maiden."

Endora studied the dart before her face fell. "This is certainly one of Aphra's darts, but that still does not explain why she would wish to kill you."

"She assisted in the murder of Lord Herod, and when we thought to find his killers she tried to end our lives," Xander told her.

Endora grasped the dart tightly in one hand and pursed her lips. "I see. That is a tale I can well believe." She straightened and glared at us. "We thank you for your information, but request that you not travel to the Coven Caves again."

My mouth dropped open. "But we didn't-" Xander drew his arm across me.

"We swear it," he promised.

Endora bowed her head and turned away. The witches melted into the dark forest.

Spiros turned to us and raised an eyebrow. "You must have an interesting tale to tell."

Euclid stretched his arm across Spiros's shoulders and grinned. "And I shall regale you with all of my bravery, old friend. It is enough to fill a tome."

"You wish to list so many falsehoods then do you intend to follow us back to Alexandria, Lord Euclid?" Spiros asked him.

Euclid shook his head. "I'll follow you as far as the foot of the mountains, but my trail leads to Bear Bay. I've heard a lot of human artifacts are going through that port lately, and I'd like a little piece of them myself."

Spiros smiled. "That will be far enough."

A dazzling light interrupted our jovial mood. I looked to the east and watched as the sun rose into the clear sky. The long night was over, and so was our adventure. I leaned against Xander's shoulder as he stood beside me and looked up into his face. "You still owe me a vacation."

He smiled and looked out over the horizon. "I have been thinking of taking you to the sea."

I closed my eyes and sighed. "Now *that* sounds like fun."

And it *was* fun, and adventurous, and terrifying, and a story for another time.

A note from Mac

Thank you for purchasing my book! Your support means a lot to me, and I'm grateful to have the opportunity to entertain you with my stories.

If you'd like to continue reading the series, or wonder what else I might have up my writer's sleeve, feel free to check out my website at *macflynn.com*, or contact me at mac@macflynn.com.

* * *

Want to get an email when the next book is released? Sign up for the Wolf Den, the online newsletter with a bite, at *eepurl.com/tm-vn*!

Continue the adventure

Now that you've finished the book, feel free to check out my website at **macflynn.com** for the rest of the exciting series.

Here's also a little sneak-peek at the next book:

Oceans Beneath Dragons:

CHAPTER 1

I lifted my chin in the air and closed my eyes. The sweet smell of salt air hit my nostrils and tingled my senses. I wrinkled my nose and let out a soft sneeze.
"Find peace," Xander spoke up.
I glanced to my left where my dragon lord rode beside me. Behind us was a short caravan of guards and Captain Spiros. The scenery around us was one of green beauty. Well-spaced trees cooled us with their branches and soft tufts of grass eased the trot of our horses as we traveled along a flat, wide trail. Sunlight lit up patches of the forest, and here and there hung thick vines. A few birds sat in the branches and sang their cooing songs to us.
I arched an eyebrow at Xander. "I might be able to find peace here, but these bugs have got to go." I winced and slapped my neck. A miss.

He smiled. "It is an old phrase that blesses you and keeps the demons from inhabiting the space just vacated by your sneeze."

My eyes widened. "Ooh, right. Like saying 'gesundheit.'"

It was his turn to give me a blank expression. "I do not know that phrase. Is it from a different language than your own?"

I nodded. "Yeah, it's German."

"And that is not your own?" he wondered.

I shook my head. "No. I speak English." I paused and furrowed my brow. "Now that I think of it, everyone in this world seems to speak my language."

Xander nodded. "Yes. The Portal has granted us constant communication to your world. Where the sus have lacked in their transference of culture, the Maidens have provided."

"What do the Maidens have to do with language?" I asked him.

Spiros eased up along my right side. "The Maidens, though captured like slaves, have always been held in high esteem by the nobility. They in turn have mimicked the Maidens' language, and that was then passed down to the people."

"Huh. Language is a funny thing," I commented. A sharp pain in my neck made me wince and slap the spot. A soft 'splat' noise told me I was successful. I drew my hand away and stuck out my tongue when I saw the sticky substance of bug goop on my palm. I wiped the muck on my jeans and glanced at Xander. "You know what's not funny is all these bugs. Are we almost out of this sweltering jungle?"

Xander stood on his stirrups and looked ahead of us without stopping. A small smile curled onto his lips. "I believe your wish has been granted."

I mimicked his movements and watched our destination come into view. The trees parted and opened into a long field that stretched for five miles. In those miles was tall, wheat-like grass that waved in the salty breeze. Small stones houses with thatched roof dotted the landscape, and low stone walls bordered the road and divided the grass-rich plains into small squares. Sheep, cows, horses, and a few other beasts I didn't recognize roamed among the stone walls chewing on the wealth of grass. Little country lanes connected the houses, and on either side of their picturesque dirt paths were tall, elegantly cut trees.

At the end of the five miles the greenery was slowly transformed into beach. Pockets of white sand mixed with the grass until there was pockets of beach grass mixed with the sand. Beyond the white lay a vast expanse of blue-green water that twinkled in the dimming daylight.

I took in the view and found myself breathless. "Wow. . ." I murmured.

Xander smiled. "Cayden will be pleased with your response."

I plopped back down onto my saddle and returned my attention to Xander. "Can all dragon lords afford to have a home on the beach like Cayden?"

"Our ancient lines do denote a certain amount of wealth, but some of us were more fortunate with the lands we inherited," he admitted as he swept his eyes over the scenery. "Cayden was fortunate to inherit the southeastern coast with its wealth of beaches and farmland."

A teasing smile slipped onto my lips. "So you're saying you don't have one?"

Xander pursed his lips and shifted in his saddle. "Not at the present, no."

I grinned and looked ahead. "So when are Cayden and Stephanie supposed to meet us here?"

"Lord Cayden will be here in a day or two. He was delayed with certain problems along the coast south of here," Spiros told me.

Xander glanced at his captain. "Have you heard what comprised these problems?"

Spiros nodded. "I have heard that a crude tribe of humans have been raiding the coastline. They take the animals from the fields and drive them onto their ships."

Xander raised an eyebrow. "But they do not take the wheat from the granaries?"

Spiros shook his head. "No."

My dragon lord pursed his lips. "That is very unusual."

"Why is it unusual?" I spoke up. "Maybe they don't like grains."

"Grains are easier to take away, particularly on ships, and grains are more difficult to grow on the islands they inhabit," he pointed out.

I tightened my grip on the reins and looked ahead. "Well, I'm not going to let a couple of raids spoil my vacation."

I kicked my heels against the sides of my horse and spurred the steed into a fast gallop. The wind whipped at my long hair as the others in our group hurried after me. The nose on Xander's horse matched mine and exceeded it.

I grinned and ducked low in the saddle. "I'm not going to let you win that easily."

A quick kick and my horse leapt into an all-out sprint. The world flew by in hues of green and blue. The hooves of my stead pounded the hard grass in quick beats. I laughed as the horse's mane brushed against my face.

Xander came up beside me and we burst into the field area together. We came up to one of the thatched cottages. A short wall surrounded the yard, and a small gate led from the yard onto the road. The gate swung open and a small boy with short wings on his back rushed into the road.

My eyes widened. I drew back and yanked on the reins. The horse whinnied and slid to a stop a few feet short of the boy. I didn't. Motion propelled me over the horn of the saddle and onto the road between the boy and my horse. I landed hard on my rear and winced as a sharp pain ran up my spine.

Xander stopped before I did and leapt down. He rushed over and knelt beside me. "Are you unhurt?"

I sat up and nodded. "Everything but my pride." I glanced over at the boy. He couldn't have been more than five and stared at us with wide eyes. "You should watch where you're going, kid."

"Colin? Colin, where are you?" a female voice cried out. A woman flew from the house and saw us on the other side of the wall. Her face turned ashen and she picked up her dress before she rushed over to us. "What's happened? Where's my-" She reached the gate and her eyes fell on the little boy. Her eyebrows crashed down. She put her hands on her hips and glared down at the young lad. "Colin, what in the world have you done now?"

His wings quivered as he shook his head. "Nothing, Mother, I swear it! I was only going out into the road to see what was all the commotion-"

"And you ran right out without looking again, didn't you?" she scolded him.

"It's all right," I spoke up as Xander helped me to my feet. I smiled at mother and son. "I shouldn't have been riding that fast, anyway."

The woman swept her eyes over our little caravan. Her attention stopped on the cloaks worn by the guards, and the symbol of Xander's house that peeked out from the clothing. She clasped her hands in front of herself and bowed her head. "I am truly sorry, Your Lordship. He's a naughty child who-"
"It's quite all right," Xander assured her. He knelt down in front of the lad who turned to face him. "How old are you?"
The lad perked up and stood as tall as his three-foot height would allow him. "I'll be six come this harvest."
Xander smiled and reached into his cloak. He drew out a small wooden whistle. "Then here is an early present for you."
The boy's face lit up as he took the gift. "Really? All for me?"
"Only if you promise to whistle before you run out into the road," Xander told him.
Colin nodded. "I will! I promise!"
"Then it is yours."
Xander handed Colin the little toy. The boy put the mouth of the whistle to his lips and blew. Its shrill call echoed over the road and yard. He lifted his head and grinned at Xander. "I bet I can get the whole of the beach to hear this! Especially from the cliffs!"
"What do you say to the kind lord?" his mother scolded him.
Colin bowed his head. "Thank you so much!" He ran off down the road.
"Don't go off to the beach! We'll go there tomorrow!" his mother called after him.
Xander stood and looked to the woman. "He is a fine boy."
His mother watched him and shook her head as a small smile danced across her lips. "Yes, and so much

like his father." She returned her attention to us and bowed her head. "I do apologize for the trouble, Your Lordship, and thank you very much for the gift."

Xander shook his head. "There was no trouble, and I can procure more of whistles."

"But it was still very good of you to do that for my little boy," she persisted.

"My Lord, there is still a ways for us to travel," Spiros spoke up.

The woman gasped and stepped back into her yard. "I beg your pardon, My Lord. I won't keep you any longer." She bowed one last time before she hurried into the house.

Xander turned away from the scene and climbed into his saddle. "Where did you get the whistle?" I asked him as I mounted my steed.

He grabbed his reins and turned his horse toward the beach. "I crafted it."

I stared at him as he trotted past me. "You crafted it? Like you made it?"

Spiros came up beside me and there was a teasing smile on his lips. "Our Lord is quite the whittler, though he denies it. So great was his love of carving that his father once suggested he be apprenticed to a carpenter."

Xander stopped his horse and looked over his shoulder at us. "Will you talk all day there or may we continue on?"

Spiros grinned and bowed his head. "Whatever you say, My Lord Whittler." I snorted as we trotted down the road to our nice, long, relaxing vacation.

If only it had turned out that way.

Other series by Mac Flynn

Contemporary Romance
Being Me
Billionaire Seeking Bride
The Family Business
Loving Places
PALE Series
Trapped In Temptation

Demon Romance
Ensnare: The Librarian's Lover
Ensnare: The Passenger's Pleasure
Incubus Among Us
Lovers of Legend
Office Duties
Sensual Sweets
Unnatural Lover

Dragon Romance
Maiden to the Dragon

Ghost Romance
Phantom Touch

Vampire Romance
Blood Thief
Blood Treasure
Vampire Dead-tective
Vampire Soul

Werewolf Romance
Alpha Blood
Alpha Mated
Beast Billionaire
By My Light
Desired By the Wolf
Falling For A Wolf
Garden of the Wolf
Highland Moon
In the Loup
Luna Proxy
Marked By the Wolf
Moon Chosen
Continued on next page
Moon Lovers
Oracle of Spirits
Scent of Scotland: Lord of Moray
Shadow of the Moon
Sweet & Sour
Wolf Lake

Manufactured by Amazon.ca
Bolton, ON